MANDY OXENDINE

Edited by

CHARLES HACKENBERRY

Foreword by

WILLIAM L. ANDREWS

Mandy Oxendine

A Novel by

CHARLES W. CHESNUTT

UNIVERSITY OF ILLINOIS PRESS

URBANA AND CHICAGO

Foreword and Introduction © 1997 by the Board of
Trustees of the University of Illinois
The novel *Mandy Oxendine* appears by permission of the
Special Collections Department of Fisk University,
Nashville, Tennessee.
Manufactured in the United States of America
1   2   3   4   5   C   P   5   4   3   2   1

This book is printed on acid-free paper.

Library of Congress Cataloging-in-Publication Data
Chesnutt, Charles Waddell, 1858–1932.
Mandy Oxendine : a novel / by Charles W. Chesnutt ;
edited by Charles Hackenberry ; foreword by William L.
Andrews.
p.   cm.
ISBN 0-252-02051-0. — ISBN 0-252-06347-3 (paper)
1. Afro-American women—Southern States—Fiction.
I. Hackenberry, Charles, 1939–   . II. Title.
PS1292.C6M26   1997
813'.4—dc20   93-553
CIP

To the memory of
Charles R. Hackenberry

Contents

Foreword

WILLIAM L. ANDREWS

Mandy Oxendine is Charles W. Chesnutt's first novel, though it has had to wait one hundred years to find a publisher. The leading African American fiction writer at the turn of the century, Chesnutt apparently began *Mandy Oxendine* a few years after he made his initial literary success as a short story writer for the prestigious *Atlantic Monthly.* Failing to interest his publisher in *Mandy Oxendine,* Chesnutt decided to focus his energies on making a book of short fiction, an effort that was doubly rewarded in 1899 with the publication of *The Conjure Woman* and *The Wife of His Youth and Other Stories of the Color Line. Mandy Oxendine* returned to its creator's file of unpublished manuscripts; evidently Chesnutt never placed it in circulation again.

The effect of *Mandy Oxendine* on the long evolution of *The House behind the Cedars* (1900), Chesnutt's first published novel, was significant, for in both stories the central issue is the dilemmas a fair-skinned African American woman must confront in passing for white. When compared with *Mandy Oxendine, The House behind the Cedars* has greater narrative density and is more sure-handed in its development of secondary characters and plots. On the other hand, with regard to the depiction of the mixed-race woman, the central figure in both stories, the earlier unpublished novel is more resistant to popular notions of femininity and less willing to accommodate itself to the protocols of "tragic mulatta" fiction than is *The House behind the Cedars*. Perhaps the fate of *Mandy Oxendine* helped convince Chesnutt that to get his version of the novel of passing into print, he would have to tone down and conventionalize some of the qualities that make Mandy Oxendine remarkable. Certainly next to Rena Walden, the pathetic ingenue who plays the victimized heroine in *The House behind the Cedars*, Mandy Oxendine seems almost italicized by her bold self-assertiveness and her canny sense of how a woman of color must operate if she is to protect and advance her interests in the post-Reconstruction South. Through her plainspoken southern vernacular, Mandy Oxendine articulates a tough-minded assessment of her racial, gendered, and class-bound condition, which sheds a good deal of light on her creator's firsthand experience of life along the color line in a region of North Carolina very much like Mandy's own milieu.

Whether Chesnutt agrees with Mandy's solution to her situation or whether he favors the strategy espoused by her eventual husband, Tom Lowrey, is left deliberately vague in *Mandy Oxendine*. In the later published novels, Chesnutt usually states or strongly implies his moral perspective on social issues, but in *Mandy Oxendine* he seems more reticent, as though testing the waters. He may have been trying to determine for himself just how far a writer in his position should go in representing forthrightly and objectively the complex web of personal desire, racial obligation, and socioeconomic ambition that held the mixed-blood in social suspension in the post–Civil War South. Is Mandy Oxendine to be condemned for having spun her own web of deceit, or has she always been caught in a cage designed by the new southern social order to restrain those who might challenge its official deceptions about color and class? However a reader responds to these questions, one suspects that the social and gender issues that probably caused *Mandy Oxendine* to seem beyond the pale one hundred years ago are likely to make the novel of more than passing interest today, for *Mandy Oxendine* is a prototype of a new brand of African American literary realism in the early twentieth century.

Introduction

CHARLES HACKENBERRY

Mandy Oxendine is, in the words Charles W. Chesnutt used to describe another of his novels, "a story of a colored girl who passed for white."[1] One of his miscegenation stories, it is probably the most important of his novels that were not published during his lifetime.[2]

Chesnutt was well suited to write about the problems of mulattos in America. His mixed racial identity gave him the experience to understand those who were resented by blacks and whites and who lived in a frustrating social position, isolated from both races.[3] Often mistaken for white, Chesnutt knew well the temptation to pass, because he wanted to succeed on the terms established by white America, yet his strong moral code would not allow him such equivocation except as a brief experiment during his youth.

Succinctly stated, *Mandy Oxendine* is the story of two fair-skinned lovers of mixed racial ancestry who have chosen to live on opposite sides of the color line. Tom Lowrey, before the opening of the narrative, takes the more conservative route to opportunity in American society of the 1880s: he leaves home to begin his higher education. Convinced that Tom has deserted her, Mandy Oxendine tries a more immediate and daring method of advancing herself: she moves to another southern community and lives as a white woman. At the completion of his studies, Tom locates Mandy and then secures a teaching position in a black school near her in order to renew his courtship. Once there, however, he learns that she has developed a new romantic interest and that she has been passing.

Chesnutt opens the tale with Tom's arrival in Mandy's community. During the interval between Mandy's going to Rosinville and Tom's appearance there, she has been courted by Robert Utley, a ne'er-do-well member of the local aristocracy. Tom's attempt to regain his former place in Mandy's heart is frustrated by the societal rules that strictly prohibit any social contact between them and by the presence of Utley. Mandy mistakenly believes that her white suitor's intentions are honorable, that he will ask for her hand and thus provide the opportunity she feels is rightly hers because she is white in appearance—if not by the racial code of the South at the end of the nineteenth century.

When Utley is killed in the act of sexually assaulting the heroine, the work takes a decided turn in the direction of the mystery genre. At the beginning of the story, the reader is caught up in Tom's struggle to regain his lost love, to advance himself, and to resolve the problems thrust upon him by a society patently intractable in all matters of race, especially those having to do with courtship and marriage. Toward the end, however, the story shows much more concern with plot than with character or theme. Will the lovers be reunited? Who actually committed the murder?

But the work is a mystery in more than its plot. When was it written? Why was it never published? From what materials and experiences did it grow?

The roots of the *Mandy Oxendine* story are sunk deeply into Chesnutt's early life and his desire to write fiction. As early as 1875, while he held his first teaching position at the age of seventeen, Chesnutt was beginning to turn the incidents of his daily life into narratives in his sporadically kept journals. The young backwoods schoolteacher was already learning in his diary to delineate character and to point his narratives toward a dramatic climax. Interspersed with observations on the conditions in rural schools, anecdotes about his students, and his thoughts on corporal punishment—all material that would find its way into the texture of *Mandy Oxendine*—are his lovesick longings for the young woman he had left behind in Charlotte. Chesnutt identifies her only as Josie C. As he worked on *Mandy Oxendine* more than twenty years later, he would draw upon a great deal of his experience during that summer of 1875 when he taught at the Macedonia schoolhouse in Beach Springs Township near Spartanburg, South Carolina.

But a considerable literary apprenticeship had yet to be completed before Chesnutt would write the novel based on his early teaching experiences. He continued to record his life in his journals, worked on short stories, and articulated his literary principles. His journal entry of 29 May 1880 shows that the serious young man of twenty-two had already arrived at the combination of literary and moral purposes that would underlie most of his mature work:

> The object of my writings would not be so much the elevation of the colored people as the elevation of the whites—for I consider the unjust spirit of caste which is so insidious as to pervade a whole nation, and so powerful as to subject a whole race and all connected with it to scorn and social ostracism—I consider this a barrier to the moral progress of the American people: and I would be one of the first to head a determined, organized crusade against it. . . . This work is of a two-fold character. The Negro's part is to prepare himself for recognition and equality, and it is the province of literature to open the way for him to get it—to accustom the public mind to the idea; and while amusing them, to lead people out, imperceptibly, unconsciously, step by step, to the desired state of feeling. If I can do anything to further this work, and can [see] any likelihood of obtaining success, I would gladly devote my life to the work.[4]

Chesnutt's last sentence merits close examination. His conditional statement, "If I can . . . [see] any likelihood of obtaining success," must be viewed in the context of his professional ambitions. While the statement certainly refers to a hoped-for success in his ability to "lead people out . . . to the desired state of feeling," it refers equally to his desire to make a comfortable living with his pen. In *Mandy Oxendine,* perhaps more obviously than in any of his works after *The Conjure Woman* (1899), Chesnutt was clearly trying to "open the way . . . while amusing" his audience at the same time. In *The Conjure Woman,* Chesnutt sought to amuse with a subtle interplay of character and the allure of myth and folklore; in *Mandy Oxendine,* the entertainment comes in the form of a cliff-hanging plot.

After his experience in rural southern schools, Chesnutt took a better position in the Normal School at Fayetteville, established for the training of black teachers. By the age of twenty-four he had become the headmaster, married a fellow teacher, begun a family, and received his first rejection slip.[5] He continued writing fiction during this period, but most of his energies went toward educating both his students and himself. By 1883 Chesnutt realized that he had progressed as far as social conditions in North Carolina would allow. After a brief period in New York City, he moved to Cleveland, secured a position with the Nickel Plate Railroad Company, and moved his family north to join him.

From 1885 to 1889 Chesnutt saw no fewer than thirty-five of his short pieces of fiction published in periodicals. In 1885 he received ten dollars from the *Cleveland News and Herald* for his first story in print, "Uncle Peter's House." In 1887 he passed the Ohio bar exam and also saw his story "The Goophered Grapevine" published in the August issue of the *Atlantic*. By 1889 he was considering another change of profession. He wrote seeking advice from George Washington Cable, one of the best-known and most-respected American men of letters of his day, whose acquaintance Chesnutt had made shortly before. Chesnutt apparently chose Cable because this white writer was himself pleading the case of African Americans in his fiction: "My object in writing to you is to inquire what is your opinion as to the wisdom, or rashness, of my adopting literature as a means of support. . . . I can turn my hand to several kinds of literary work, can write a story, a funny skit, can turn a verse, and write a serious essay. I have even written a novel, though it has never seen the light, nor been offered to a publisher."[6]

DATE OF COMPOSITION

Exactly which novel manuscript Chesnutt was referring to in his 1889 letter to Cable is now impossible to tell. *The House behind the Cedars* (1900), his first published novel, seems a likely choice, but another letter between the two men during 1889 rules out this possibility.[7] That narrative was still of short story length and Chesnutt continued to call it "Rena Walden."

Through the late 1880s Chesnutt published more short fiction. The *Atlantic* took two additional stories, "Po Sandy" in May 1888 and "Dave's Neckliss" in October 1889. During the early 1890s, while his legal and stenographic business provided him and his family with an increasingly comfortable living, he resumed work on a novel. In 1895 he again wrote to Cable about his fiction: "I thank you for the kind suggestion that I again enter the literary field. I have never abandoned it in fact. . . . But I wrote last year a novel of about 60,000 to 70,000 words. I had not completed my revision of it when the Fall business came on with a rush, and diverted me from it. I expect ere the Summer is over to finish it."[8] In the same letter Chesnutt mentions that the "Rena" story, clearly another work, had grown to between 25,000 and 28,000 words. If the novel Chesnutt is referring to is *Mandy Oxendine,* he either shortened the piece considerably as it neared final form or else he greatly overestimated the length of the work, for the manuscript as it exists barely reaches 40,000 words, the somewhat arbitrary border between a novella and a novel.

The most telling piece of evidence that relates to when *Mandy Oxendine* was written is the cover letter, dated 13 February 1897, that Chesnutt sent to Walter Hines Page, an editor who had helped and encouraged him earlier. In it Chesnutt suggests that the work be considered for periodical publication in the *Atlantic* or for book publication by Houghton Mifflin.[9] In about six weeks he received his answer, but it could hardly have been the one he had hoped for.

> Dear Sir,
>
> We read Mandy Oxendine for the Atlantic and then considered it, at your request, for book publication, and we are sorry that we must now return you the ms. as unavailable in either form for our use. We do not publish many novels, and though we recognize elements of truthfulness, and some novelty of situation in this, we are not able to persuade ourselves that we should find publication a safe venture.[10]

If Chesnutt later sought publication for the work elsewhere, no record of his efforts has survived. By the time he received his letter of rejection, he was already working on several short stories and his ongoing revision of "Rena." Perhaps he felt that *The House behind the Cedars* would say all he cared to about passing and intermarriage, or perhaps he suspected that his collections of short stories would be much better received. Whatever his reasons, Chesnutt seems to have taken little interest in *Mandy Oxendine* after it was refused by Houghton Mifflin in the early spring of 1897.

It seems safe to conclude that *Mandy Oxendine* was probably finished early in 1897, that 1896 may indeed be a more reasonable estimate of the completion date, and that the work may have been started in 1894—though it possibly could have existed, in one form or another, as early as 1889. In any case, *Mandy Oxendine* is almost certainly Chesnutt's earliest extant novel.

Many passages in Chesnutt's unpublished journals, especially those written during the time he was teaching at the Macedonia school, seem to have provided him with both the central ideas for particular characters and the phrases and pronunciations that would help him create the dialogue in *Mandy Oxendine*. "Over half my scholars err in the alphabet. I tried singing this morning. They said they knew 'Shall We Gather &c' and I sang it. The larger girls 'Miss Louisa Peak' &c whined it through their noses in a decidedly droll manner."[11] Chesnutt drew many of the names used in *Mandy Oxendine* directly from his journals. Brer Revels and Brer Peak are found by name in both. Chesnutt took the first name of one of his students and combined it with the last name of another to produce a name for one of the children in Tom Lowrey's classroom. It would be a mistake, however, to assume that all the characters and incidents that appear in the novel were taken from the record of his early teaching days—or even from the recollections of those years that his journals certainly would have evoked. For example, the character finally called Elder Gadson, the "John the Baptist" minister, was modeled after one Elder Davis, whose unique ideas on preaching Chesnutt recorded some time after his summer teaching stint.[12]

Absent from the journal of 1876 are the names Mandy Oxendine and Tom Lowrey, the central characters of the novel. That is not to say that this journal provided Chesnutt no assistance in the creation of their personalities. When Chesnutt took his position in the Macedonia school, he left behind a young woman who frequently occupied his thoughts. Perhaps, given the frequency of references to her in his journals of this period, it may be more accurate to say that she obsessed his thoughts: "I was awful lonesome yesterday afternoon. Could think of nothing but Charlotte and Josie. I want to go to Spartanburg, and get my mail. There is sure to be a letter from Jo, if she's in Charlotte. But I must wait till Saturday. 'God bless you Jo!' "[13] The young woman's name crops up repeatedly in his journal that summer, and the youthful Chesnutt inscribed a love poem to her there. Many references in the journal of 1876 suggest Tom's feelings toward Mandy, but the Oxendine name, which also appears in *The House behind the Cedars* and can still be found in the Fayetteville area, is not among those the author recorded in his journals of this period.

Though several minor characters came directly from Chesnutt's journals, the principal characters were more imaginatively conceived.

Surely his recollections of the young woman he had left behind would have helped him create Mandy, but it is unlikely that Chesnutt worked directly from life in any large measure. Certainly he would have found the image of himself as a young man in a strange rural community helpful in bringing Tom Lowrey to life.

The parallels between Charles Chesnutt and Tom Lowrey are many. Both are young men who moved to rural school districts in the South to accept brief summer teaching positions. Both are of mixed racial ancestry, and both are taken for white.[14] But the differences cannot be overlooked. Lowrey, though young, seems older than Chesnutt was in 1875—he was just turning seventeen when the summer session began. Lowrey, though believed to be white when he arrives in Rosinville, North Carolina, has reached a firm decision to live on the black side of the area's strict color line. As the journal entries of 1875 clearly show, Chesnutt in his mid-teens was still considering the alternatives: "Twice today, or oftener, I have been taken for 'white.' At the pond this morning one fellow said 'he'd be damned if there was any nigger blood in me.' At Coleman's I passed. On the road, on old chap, seeing the trunks, took me for a student coming from school. I believe I'll leave here and pass anyhow, for I am as white as any of them."[15] But in the novel that grew from Chesnutt's experiences of this period, passing for white is the daring route to opportunity taken by the heroine, not by Tom Lowrey.

While Chesnutt's journals for 1875 through 1880 would no doubt have helped him develop characters, create dialogue, and sketch local color, the mature writer twenty years later did not attempt simply to relate the events of his young life in a fictional mode, as had earlier black writers such as Harriet E. Wilson. Instead, Chesnutt used his journals much as Thoreau used his as he wrote *Walden*, taking the details of his daily life, his experiences, but casting them in ways that reflect, even if they do not mirror precisely, the world in which he lived.

CRITICAL EVALUATION

The world presented in *Mandy Oxendine* is rigidly structured, with the color line as the most obvious and important delineator of "caste," a favorite term of Chesnutt's, who included within it the prejudice toward mixed bloods as well as toward blacks and the denial of opportunities to both. At the beginning of the story, Mandy's decision to cross the color line has severed her ties with most of her family and former friends, as would Rena Walden's similar decision in *The House behind the Cedars*.

Mandy is willing to pay such a price for she has learned to be pragmatic: "A person has got to be white or black in this world, an' I ain't goin' to be black." For her, opportunity—and this is the key word of the novel—presents itself as the possibility of marriage to a white man, a fallen Carolinian aristocrat, to whom Mandy has no intention of telling her secret. Perhaps this is what the editor at Houghton Mifflin meant in 1897 when, in rejecting the piece, he noted that the work had "some novelty of situation." Indeed, in its day, only a decade after the violence accompanying the collapse of Reconstruction, *Mandy Oxendine* would have been considered shocking. Chesnutt's endorsement of such a route to opportunity would have offended almost all of the white reading public, no matter how successful his method of amusement.

Tom Lowrey's route to opportunity is much more conservative. Like Chesnutt, he chooses education for both his livelihood and his means to rise above his caste. To a large degree, the choices made by Tom and Mandy, education and passing, symbolize two of the three paths to opportunity open to southern men and women of mixed racial ancestry. The third path, moving to the North, is offered as a possibility at the end of the story.

Through the events of the novel, Chesnutt sanctions all three means of personal advancement and implies the appropriateness of each in late nineteenth-century American society. The outcome of his characters' lives reveals, in most of his other fiction as well as in *Mandy Oxendine*, that Chesnutt believed that those who invest in their talents and those who are virtuous (by his standards) fare well in life no matter what their color. The exception comes when violence or tragedy ends a life prematurely. To a degree, Mandy Oxendine and Tom Lowrey prefigure Josh Green and Dr. Miller, two symbolic characters in *The Marrow of Tradition* (1901), a work that brought the wrath of the conservative white critical establishment down firmly on Chesnutt's tender ego and his even more fragile literary career. Mandy's means are as extreme as Josh Green's—less violent, but much more insidious and almost impossible for the dominant white culture to counter. One can only imagine the controversy *Mandy Oxendine* would have stirred up, and the consequent effects on Chesnutt's budding literary career, had the editors at Houghton Mifflin decided to publish this slim novel in 1897.

Chesnutt's handling of plot is important to the book's theme: what happens to the heroine represents an authorial comment on her attempted method of assimilation. Though Mandy is accused of murder and is imprisoned, she escapes both rape and a death sentence through

the interposition of a minister and a teacher. Tom's fate is equally significant. His nobility makes him offer to take Mandy's place on the gallows,
but he too escapes punishment for a crime he did not commit.

In a truly whirlwind finish, the lovers are reunited, married, and
whisked away to an unknown (though presumably happy) future:
"Whether they went to the North, where there was larger opportunity
and a more liberal environment, and remaining true to their own people, in spite of some scorn and some isolation, found a measurable
degree of contentment and happiness; or whether they chose to sink
their past in the gulf of oblivion, and sought in the great white world
such a place as their talents and their virtues merited, it is not for this
chronicle to relate. They deserved to be happy. . . ."

For all its excellent details of dialect and local color, and despite the
importance of its racial themes, *Mandy Oxendine* is not a completely
successful marriage of "amusement" and "elevation." Its shift of focus,
from a story of character and theme to a story of plot, strains the work.
The exploration of appropriate ways to gain equality, as important as
this is to the book's message, is put aside when the novel starts to become
a mystery. Several of Chesnutt's unpublished novels testify to his desire
to write popular fiction. His introduction of a popularizing device, the
mystery form, two-thirds of the way into *Mandy Oxendine* dilutes its
themes of injustice and thwarted opportunity.

As William L. Andrews has observed, in *Mandy Oxendine* Chesnutt
pays little attention to the inner lives of his main characters and to the
delineation of their social environment. The only critic to have written
about the work at any length, Andrews also recognizes that it is "essentially a long short story,"[16] and this, to some extent, explains its weakness
as a novel. A. Robert Lee has pointed out that Chesnutt's best work is his
short fiction and that his longer works are strained when they attempt to
educate and entertain simultaneously.[17] By 1896 Chesnutt had published
no book-length fiction. His greatest successes until then were his stories
in the *Atlantic*. His first two volumes of fiction, both appearing in 1899,
were collections of stories. In *Mandy Oxendine*, Chesnutt had not yet
found a consistent way to accommodate both of his aims without weak-
ening the contexture and significance of the work; the reader's interest
in the story line is heightened at the expense of the narrative's racial
themes.

Juggling the elements of an exciting plot while trying to focus the
reader's attention on his thematic concerns was not Chesnutt's only
problem in his first novel. Quite simply, the narrator of *Mandy Ox-*

endine speaks with the too-studied correctness and formality of the hero. A similar condition exists in *The Conjure Woman,* but in that work the contrast between the resonant wit of Uncle Julius and the stuffy formality of the first-person narrator of the outer frame story, a well-to-do conservative northerner who buys a plantation after the Civil War, enlivens the piece and underscores its dramatic tension. Given the newcomer's rather stodgy attitudes, diction, and phrasing, the reader of *The Conjure Woman* is amused at John's powerlessness, his inability to win a contest of wills and intelligence with Uncle Julius. In *Mandy Oxendine,* the formal tone of the narrator is not balanced by a more down-to-earth voice. Instead, the reader continues to listen to one idiolect that, while it is never dreary or monotonous, is certainly not as amusing or various as those in *The Conjure Woman.*

That Chesnutt fell somewhat short of finding a voice that would fully persuade the reader of the rightness of his major theme is no final measure of the value of his work. Nor does it undercut the importance of the book. When *Mandy Oxendine* is seen beside the other race fiction of its day, and especially that which immediately preceded it, Chesnutt's shortcomings in his first novel diminish and his accomplishments become much clearer.

Evolving from the slave narrative and the eighteenth-century novel, book-length fiction written by African Americans was already beginning to form a literary tradition by the time Chesnutt considered embarking on a full-time career in letters. William Wells Brown's *Clotel; or, The President's Daughter,* the first published novel by a black American, appeared in 1853 (five years before Chesnutt was born), and Frank J. Webb's *The Garies and Their Friends* was brought out in 1857—both in England. Harriet E. Wilson's *Our Nig,* the first novel by an African American to be published in the United States, was privately printed by the author in 1859. But to these and later black novels of the nineteenth century, such as Frances E. W. Harper's *Iola Leroy; or, Shadows Uplifted* (1892), *Mandy Oxendine* bears only limited resemblance. Unlike Brown, Chesnutt was not so much interested in establishing the causes behind social conditions as he was in showing the effects of those conditions on nonwhite men and women of talent and temperament, among whom he doubtless counted himself. The realism of Chesnutt's first novel is very different from the sentimentalism of some earlier works by African-American authors; missing from *Mandy Oxen-*

dine is the gratuitous malevolence of a white overseer character, though the lower-class whites of the lynching episode approach the stereotype. Nowhere in his book does Chesnutt try to document the factual elements of his fiction, a characteristic of many earlier black novels that shows their roots in both slave and abolitionist narratives. What Chesnutt drew from the black tradition in fiction, a feature quite observable in Wilson's *Our Nig,* was the thesis that men and women of color are fully human, possessed of hopes and fears—every bit as eager as whites to control their own destinies and just as capable of doing so successfully. Chesnutt contributed to this tradition by creating characters, sometimes black but usually of mixed racial ancestry, who are willing to risk the consequences of opposing racial prejudice and are bold enough to seize opportunities for advancement wherever they can be found.

Chesnutt wanted to write popular race fiction, a field dominated by white writers. Black novelists like Pauline Hopkins and Sutton Griggs had the attention of only a small percentage of the novel-buying public, and Chesnutt envisioned greater sales for his books than these writers were able to generate for their own. He also wanted to write fiction that presented nonwhites honestly—and thus change the racial attitudes of whites—but it was just as important that he earn a comfortable living from the sale of his books. An assessment of his work cannot overlook either of these aims.

From the start of his career, Chesnutt felt that he could fulfill his ambitions by writing race fiction that was both entertaining and realistic. Many of his major nonwhite characters, though certainly not all, are complex portraits of human beings endowed with intelligence and a broad range of abilities—very different from the black and mulatto characters that people the more popular race fiction of Chesnutt's day and the period immediately preceding it. The primary reason for this difference is that those who were truly Chesnutt's competitors in the literary marketplace, even those who espoused enfranchisement and education for the minority, had no experience living on the darker side of the color line.

Albion Winegar Tourgée and George Washington Cable were both sensitive to the conditions under which southern blacks suffered during the period. A southerner by birth, Cable knew intimately the circumstances he wrote about; Tourgée lacked Cable's firsthand experience, but before moving to North Carolina in 1865 he traveled widely and studied deeply, advocating education as the chief means for reform. They shared a humanitarian impulse that led them to plead the case of the oppressed and to oppose with their fiction those attitudes they considered morally wrong. Such highminded principles were not the rule, however, for every writer of that literary form which became a quite lucrative commercial enterprise. Thomas Dixon, who wrote somewhat later, capitalized on a strong undercurrent of fear and resentment among whites, and Thomas Nelson Page profited by tapping into a desire to return to things irretrievably past, most particularly antebellum plantation society. Blacks were, according to Page, entirely unfit for both freedom and personal responsibility.

When Page set his fiction in the Reconstruction period, his racism grew very strong. *Red Rock* (1898) makes it clear that the only "good" blacks are those who know their servile place and keep it. Those who do not are portrayed as corrupt legislators, overemotional preachers, and quacks. Page uses distorted physical descriptions to "prove" that blacks constituted a subspecies, grotesque creatures somewhere in the great chain of being between true men (whites) and beasts.

Chesnutt's fiction is a corrective to that written by Page. Both Tom Lowrey and Mandy Oxendine are unhappy with the meager portion that southern society has allowed them. They want to choose for themselves what to make of their talents and lives. Mandy, in particular, is not to be held back by the opinions or mores of those who would restrict her. Tom has delayed his marriage to Mandy until he is educated and established in his career. His plan is that both he and his wife will then rise to a higher social level and gain greater financial rewards. They both desire to find the positions in society that they deserve because of what they can do and who they are; they will not settle for what the aristocratic culture, which Chesnutt shows in its degeneracy, has decided is their due.

In direct contrast to what one sees in the stories of Page set during Reconstruction, the independent mulattos in *Mandy Oxendine* are morally superior to every white character and completely willing to chance the American Dream. Chesnutt draws his main characters as fully human beings, endowed with aspirations and sensibilities that are at least the equal of those of his white characters. Though Tom and Mandy may not have quite the depth and dimension of some characters created by other realistic novelists, in their psychological complexity they more closely resemble the characters developed by Stephen Crane and William Dean Howells than they do the stereotypes of Page. Chesnutt attempts to show the oppressive weight of prejudice and tradition on the individual and thus sketches the private feelings and dreams of nonwhite men and women. *Mandy Oxendine* is his first full-length disquisition on the nature of the hearts and minds of those he understood very well.

The novels of Tourgée also show concern with the plight of the Negro after the Civil War. His fiction, like that of Chesnutt, deals forthrightly with the dilemma created by Emancipation. Blacks, Tourgée rightly argued, needed more than the vote. In *Bricks without Straw* (1880), he demonstrates that education would do much to right the wrongs of slavery. An understanding of the bitterness brought about by a corrupt system, he believed, would help whites to get through a difficult period. Though Tourgée was far from Page in his opinion of blacks, Chesnutt found unacceptable Tourgée's treatment of mulattos in his fiction. As his letter to Cable shows, Chesnutt felt that racially mixed characters ought not to be presented as being dependent upon the opinion of whites for their sense of self-worth.

> Judge Tourgée's cultivated white Negroes are always bewailing their fate and cursing the drop [of] black blood which "taints"—I hate the word, it implies corruption—their otherwise pure race. An English writer would not hesitate . . . to say that race prejudice was mean and narrow and unchristian. He would not be obliged to kill off his [mulatto] characters or immure them in convents, as Tourgée does his latest heroine. . . . An English writer will make his Colored characters think no less of themselves because of their race, but infinitely less of those who despise them because of it.[18]

In *Mandy Oxendine* Chesnutt presents "white Negroes" who accept their unique position as a matter of fact. They neither curse their ancestry nor stoically accept circumstances as they find them, as did many "tragic mulatto" characters in race fiction.

Mandy believes that her right to pass comes from God, because she is white in appearance. She is free from the latent sense of inferiority that Tourgée's 'Toinette seems to feel, even when the community discovers Mandy's true racial identity, for she has a fundamental faith in herself. Moreover, her decision to pass for white brings no pangs of conscience. Her right to a better life (free of resentment from blacks because she is white in appearance; free of prejudice from whites because she is "not white enough") can be claimed because she is simply a human being. Her rights have nothing whatsoever to do with being of a "pure race"— either white or black.

Though Chesnutt later found Tourgée "a very interesting fellow . . .

[who] improves on acquaintance,"[19] he held firmly to his own views on how to depict those of mixed racial origins in his novels and short stories. Chesnutt's fiction is the first in America to treat with such realism, compassion, and perceptiveness the problems of those who looked most longingly at the opportunities on the other side of the color line. His experiences as a "voluntary Negro," a term he used to describe himself, raise his fiction above that of others whose stories treat the unique problems of the mulatto in American society, even above the tales of that fellow writer on the other side of the color barrier whose work and opinions Chesnutt most respected.

Of all the white writers who wove their fiction from the light and dark strands of racial concern that both troubled and fascinated the nation between the Civil War and the turn of the century, Cable best understood the minority. Born in New Orleans and brought up on abolitionist idealism, he had the inclination and the opportunity to observe the lives of blacks and mulattos and to study the rich history of his multicultural native region. Much of Cable's fiction demonstrates his desire to reform public attitudes on the question of race, and the correspondence between Cable and Chesnutt shows the high opinion the aspiring novelist had of the established author's accomplishments and aims.

Cable's depiction of mulattos, while more sympathetic and individualized than Tourgée's, is more highly romanticized than Chesnutt's, and his fiction that deals with intermarriage is more conservative. In "Tite Poulette," one of the stories from *Old Creole Days* (1879), Cable goes so far as to suggest that love may indeed conquer racial prejudice and tradition in a mixed marriage, but he nevertheless pulls back from showing a white American proposing to a woman of certain mixed ancestry. Such equivocation was common in fiction that dealt with the marriage of a white to a mulatto. In Rebecca Harding Davis's *What Answer?* (1869), an interracial marriage actually takes place, but the mulatto woman soon dies, ironically, in a race riot in New York. William Dean Howells in *An Imperative Duty* (1891) sends his interracial couple to Italy after their marriage.

By bringing Tom and Mandy back together at the end of the story, Chesnutt manages to keep his tale just within the limits of what popular race fiction would allow. *Mandy Oxendine* stretches the genre to its limits in other directions too: the nonwhite heroine is the potential marriage partner who seeks the union with a white man, Utley, and, as mentioned before, she plans to keep her ancestry a secret. Furthermore,

Mandy's affections are drawn back to Tom, a nonwhite, even before Utley's death. Intermarriage, Chesnutt implies, is one acceptable means of advancement, but so too is passing for white or moving to the North. Chesnutt's exploration of a whole range of solutions to the problem of repression in the South makes his fiction a much more complete and daring study.

Like Chesnutt, Cable was attacked for what readers felt was his advocacy of miscegenation, but his fictional treatment of the matter is very different from Chesnutt's. Cable sketched careful portraits of his mulatto characters, yet intermarriage was still very much a question for him. To Chesnutt, racial admixture was already a fact of American life. Racial mixing had begun shortly after the arrival of the first slaves, and Chesnutt's own experiences, talents, and ambitions led him to understand, and later to demonstrate in his fiction, that intermarriage could give birth to human beings equal to those of "pure" race. To do less would have been to deny the value of his own ancestry and to accept the opinions of the "tragic mulattos" of fiction.

The problem for Chesnutt was not whether intermarriage was right or wrong. It centered instead, he felt, on what nonwhites could do to attain equality of opportunity within a social system in which the process of racial mixing had been going on for years without sanction. For Mandy Oxendine, marrying a white man is, before Tom Lowrey returns, the only route to opportunity she has, and her right to advancement outweighs nearly everything else for her. For her breach of accepted social conduct she suffers no lasting consequences. Chesnutt's mulatto characters in *Mandy Oxendine* want, above all else, to control their own destinies. They know their society for what it is, and they refuse to accept the limitations that society would impose upon them. In their quest for freedom of opportunity, Mandy and Tom are far more modern than the characters of either Tourgée or Cable. They foreshadow the kind of self-realized nonwhite character, such as Gabriel in Arna Bontemps's *Black Thunder* (1936), that would signal a dramatic strengthening of the black self-image.

The Harlem Renaissance of the 1920s and 1930s, which grew out of a sense of racial pride and in turn nurtured that pride, gave full voice to the legitimacy of black culture and to sexual relationships between those of different races. But Chesnutt, the Victorian gentleman in many respects, never came to accept a movement so steeped in alcohol, sex, and jazz, as he perceived the Harlem Renaissance to be. In his depiction of the desires and aspirations of nonwhites, he is both more idealistic and more realistic than either Tourgée or Cable. His vision of the kind of life that it was possible for an African American to lead is loftier and more optimistic than that of many writers who gained public attention after he abandoned the literary profession.

Though Chesnutt was by nature a meliorist, Mandy Oxendine's escape from punishment for her chosen method of assimilation represents a sharp departure from what is generally considered Chesnutt's formula for success and advancement beyond the color line—education and hard work. Since *Mandy Oxendine* is an early work, this more radical strain of thought might logically be viewed as a collateral prescription, one that influenced the creation of Rena Walden in *The House behind the Cedars* and then surfaced even more forcefully in Josh Green of *The Marrow of Tradition*. In Chesnutt's later stories, his main characters are more constricted, trapped within the racist traditions of southern society; in *Mandy Oxendine,* their struggles are more successful and they are able to reach a higher level of freedom. While Chesnutt undoubtedly relies upon stereotypes of black characters to approach and amuse his intended audience, the white reading public, he nevertheless points out and endorses daring paths to opportunity for those non-whites brave and strong enough to follow them. Josh Green is killed for his rebellion, but Mandy Oxendine is married to Tom Lowrey, and their decision to live as either whites or nonwhites is concealed behind the novel's final curtain.

Those who presented the Spingarn Medal to Chesnutt in 1928 did more than bring solace to an aging, neglected author. By bestowing on him his highest public honor, they recognized long after the fact that his portraits of blacks and mulattos are important contributions to African-American fiction, that his works deal with the lives of complex individuals and not just with classes or stereotypes, and that all his books deserve to be remembered as significant contributions to American literature.

NOTE ON THE TEXT

The copy text for this edition is a single typescript, with amendments in the author's distinctive hand, located in the Charles W. Chesnutt Collection, Fisk University Library Special Collections, Nashville, Tennessee. The novel is contained in folders 1 through 4 in box 8 of the collection, the largest repository of Chesnutt's holographs and manuscripts.

The typescript covers 178 continuously paginated thin white sheets, typed more or less neatly on one side. An unnumbered initial page contains the title, the author's name in the form "Chas.W.Chesnutt," and his business address, "1024 Society for Savings Building, Cleveland, Ohio." With the exception of two words torn from the right margin of the final page, the novel is complete; "The End" appears at the foot of typescript page 178.

No other manuscript copies of *Mandy Oxendine* are known to exist, and there are no previously published editions. Information on Chesnutt's writing habits and procedures presented by his daughter, Helen M. Chesnutt, leads me to believe that the copy in the Fisk collection may not be the one the author sent to Houghton Mifflin and Co.[20] In addition to considerable work on the dialect, some major reordering of material was undertaken during the composition of this copy. Some chapters appear to have been written before Chesnutt knew exactly where they would go in the final version of the work. In two large sections of the narrative—chapters 7–15 and chapters 19–24—Chesnutt wrote the word "Chapter" at the head of a new page that was to begin a chapter and added a line on which to insert the chapter number. At a later time the numbers were added—sometimes by hand, sometimes by typewriter, and sometimes first by hand, then erased, and later typed over the erasure. Clearly, the novel was still in a fluid state at the time Chesnutt began to prepare the version that serves as the copy text for this edition.[21]

NOTES

1. Quoted in William L. Andrews, *The Literary Career of Charles W. Chesnutt* (Baton Rouge: Louisiana State University Press, 1980), p. 123.

2. "A Business Career," "The Rainbow Chasers," "Paul Marchand, F.M.C," "Evelyn's Husband," and "The Quarry" are the other unpublished novels, all in the Chesnutt Collection, Fisk University Library Special Collections (hereafter cited as Chesnutt Collection).

3. Chesnutt's racial origins are detailed in Andrews, *Literary Career of Charles W. Chesnutt*, pp. 1–2, and in Frances Richardson Keller, *An American Crusade: The Life of Charles Waddell Chesnutt* (Provo, Utah: Brigham Young University Press, 1978), p. 27.

4. Journal of 1880, p. 191, Chesnutt Collection. Citing the correct date for entries from Chesnutt's unpublished journals is troublesome because of his inconsistent dating habits. The reader should be aware that the journal dates offered here are, in some cases, quite tentative. Also, page numbers are not in Chesnutt's hand but were stamped on at a later day and are not always accurate.

5. Sylvia Lyons Render, "Introduction," in *The Short Fiction of Charles W. Chesnutt,* ed. Sylvia Lyons Render (Washington, D.C.: Howard University Press, 1974), pp. 9–10. Some of my discussion is informed by Render's introduction. For a more complete biography, see Keller, *American Crusade.*

6. Chesnutt to Cable, March 1889, Chesnutt Collection.

7. Cable to Chesnutt, 25 September 1889, Chesnutt Collection.

8. Chesnutt to Cable, 11 April 1895, Chesnutt Collection.

9. Chesnutt to Walter Hines Page, 13 February 1897, Chesnutt Collection.

10. Houghton Mifflin to Chesnutt, 26 March 1897, Chesnutt Collection.

11. Journal of 1876, p. 107, Chesnutt Collection.

12. Journal of 1877, p. 170, Chesnutt Collection.

13. Journal of 1876, p. 110, Chesnutt Collection.

14. Brer Pate believes that Lowrey is white when he meets the new teacher at the station, an opening that Chesnutt was to use again in *The Marrow of Tradition* and in a slightly different form in *The House behind the Cedars.*

15. Journal of 1876, p. 103, Chesnutt Collection.

16. Andrews, *Literary Career of Charles W. Chesnutt,* p. 146.

17. A. Robert Lee, " 'The Desired State of Feeling': Charles Waddell Chesnutt and Afro-American Literary Tradition," *Durham University Journal* 3 (1974): 165.

18. Chesnutt to Cable, 5 June 1890, Chesnutt Collection. My text for the letter is the rough draft in Chesnutt's hand rather than the carbon copy, also in the collection, which was probably prepared by Helen Chesnutt and which varies somewhat from the version given here.

19. Chesnutt to Susan Chesnutt, 20 July 1891, quoted in Helen Chesnutt, *Charles Waddell Chesnutt: Pioneer of the Color Line* (Chapel Hill: University of North Carolina Press, 1952), p. 65.

20. Helen M. Chesnutt to Elmer Adler, 29 December 1936, quoted in *Breaking into Print,* ed. Elmer Adler (New York: Simon and Schuster, 1937), pp. 47–48. In this letter Helen Chesnutt discusses the various drafts that her father prepared as he worked on his fiction. Some of the copy of *The House behind the Cedars* that accompanied her letter is described as a "first typed copy with changes and corrections which he made." A fair typed copy was customarily then prepared from the amended typed version; the typescript of *Mandy Oxendine* in the Chesnutt Collection appears to be what Helen Chesnutt describes as a "first typed copy."

21. In "A Technical Edition of Charles Chesnutt's *Mandy Oxendine*" (Ph.D. diss., Pennsylvania State University, 1982) I show all features of the typescript—cancellation, interlineation, variant readings, original pagination, and amendments. Copies are available from University Microforms, 300 North Zeeb Road, Ann Arbor, MI 48106.

Mandy Oxendine

Charles W. Chesnutt at the age of twenty-five.
(Courtesy of the Cleveland Public Library)

Chapter 1

The engine whistle shrieked long and loud, the train gradually slackened its speed, and jolting ponderously over the uneven track ran into the depot at Rosinville, North Carolina. The depot consisted of a long wooden shed, open at the sides, and wide enough for the roof to cover the railroad track and a raised platform of equal length with the shed. The platform terminated at one end in a long inclined plane, up which trucks could be run with ease, and at the other end was partitioned off for offices and waiting-room. A pile of cotton-bales, ranged in tiers, occupied a large part of the platform. On the open ground beyond, long rows of yellow rosin-barrels, encrusted with amber exudations, glistened in the ardent sunlight.

A young man alighted from the rear passenger coach—a tall young man, somewhat fair of complexion, with grey eyes and light slightly curly hair. He was clad in a loosely-fitting grey suit that had seen some wear, and carried a large and apparently heavy valise in his hand. The traveler walked across the platform, with the intention of leaving his valise in the waiting-room, but on approaching the door he noticed a sign—"This Waiting-room for White People Only." He flushed angrily, hesitated a moment, and then kept on toward the waiting-room, but paused before he reached it, and turning aside deposited the bag on the platform, where he could keep it in sight. He then looked around as though in search of some one.

There were several well-dressed people around the depot. They had evidently come to meet one of his fellow-travelers, a handsome, proud-looking young woman who had ridden on the train from the other terminus, where our traveller had got on. A lady of mature years in a stylish dress of dark cloth, and with a small black bonnet surmounting a head which time had begun to whiten, greeted the younger woman with a kiss and an embrace. The young lady, visibly unbending, returned the caress with appreciable warmth. A young girl of about sixteen and a boy of fourteen added their greetings with the exuberance of childhood, and the entire party entered a waiting carriage, drawn by two horses, and drove rapidly away.

The young man looked around among the porters and loiterers about the depot, and finally directed his steps toward an elderly negro, who had walked along the side of the passenger coaches and was now standing near the door of one of them, looking around in evident perplexity. The young man walked up to him.

"Are you looking for some one?"

"Yas, boss, I wuz a-lookin' fer a young colored man what wuz comin' in on de kyars. Did you seed any sech young man git off'n de train?"

"The teacher for Sandy Run School?"

"Yas sir. Why, how did you know!"

"I reckon I'm the man. Lowrey is my name."

"Why, laws-a-massy! Brer Lowrey, I's glad ter meet you." He looked at the young man with respectful scrutiny and then added, in a tone that indicated some uncertainty, "I beg yo' pahdun, suh, but we wuz expectin' a colored man. Is you—"

"Oh, yes, I'm all right; not very highly colored, but sufficiently so, I reckon."

"Well, I do declar'," said the old man, "I never would a dremp' you wuz de teacher. I was lookin' fer a dark man, er a yaller man f'um de secon'-class kyar. I wuz'n' lookin' fer no white gen'leman f'um de fus'-class kyar. Nobody wouldn't never b'lieve you wuz colored, ef somebody didn' tell 'em."

It was not the first time the same thing had been said to Lowrey and he heard it with a mingled feeling of pleasure and annoyance. It was a substantial advantage to have a white skin in the Southern States. But to be white in fact and black in theory was a situation not without embarrassing features. Lowrey did not pursue the subject.

"Are you Mr. Pate?" he asked.

"Dat's my name—Jeff'son Pate, er Deacon Pate, er Brer Jeff—I answers to 'mos' anythin' you min' ter call me."

"I got your letter, Mr. Pate, and I am in your hands."

"I'll take keer er you, suh. Bein' de only colored member er de school committee, I felt dat I oughter come ter meet you and take you out ter de school-house. Tain't mo' d'n a couple or fo' miles, but I thought you might hab some baggage, so I brung my kyart along. I'll go an' git yo' carpet-bag an' we'll walk over in de shade whar de mewil is hitch'."

"I'm very much obliged indeed," said Lowrey. "I won't trouble you about the bag, though."

He stepped quickly ahead of the old man, and having got his grip-sack followed the other across the dusty street to where, in the shade of a clump of elms, a two-wheeled cart stood waiting. To the cart was harnessed a sleepy looking mule, which gave no signs of animation except an occasional switch of his tufted tail to drive away the lazily swarming flies. On the cart was a basket filled with brown paper parcels, and a bag of meal, while a brown jug, fastened by a piece of twine, swung underneath the axle. A yellow dog asleep in the shade woke up at their approach and gave Lowrey a friendly sniff.

"I's done all my tradin'," said the old man, "an' less'n you wants ter look roun' de town er buy sump'n at de sto's, I's ready ter go right out."

"I'm ready and willing," said Lowrey. "I can see the town some other time."

Mr. Pate untied the mule, took the rope lines in his hands, and perched himself on one side of the cart, his feet dangling down. Lowrey took a similar position on the other side, and put up his umbrella to keep off the sun. The mule woke up, shook the flies from his long ears and started at a slow trot. The yellow dog sprang forward and for a few rods ran barking ahead of them, but soon fell back and took up a jog-trot under the cart-tail, in close proximity to the swaying jug.

The town was small, and they were soon out of it. The heat was oppressive, although it was late in the afternoon. The mule soon ceased to trot, and moved with characteristic deliberation through a rolling sand-hill country. Now and then, at the foot of an incline, he would splash into a warm branch, and stand up to his fetlocks in the clear running water, with a long drawn out pretense of drinking. The old man struck him sharply from time to time with a hickory switch, and addressed to him both argument and remonstrance; but the results were purely spasmodic. Pines, pines, pines, covered the low, rolling hills and lined the roadside—long-leaved pines, scarred with turpentine boxes; short-leaved pines of later growth, their degenerate successors, fit for nothing but a poor quality of cord-wood. A scrubby blackjack undergrowth filled the space between the pines, except where it had been cleared away for easier access to the turpentine boxes. The air was rich and heavy with the odor of the pines, and murmurous with their gentle swaying, and at times the cart moved noiselessly over a carpet of brown spikelets and fallen cones. In the hollows only, along the branches, the water-oak, small of leaf and dense of foliage, the honeysuckle, the fragrant bay-tree, the cypress—children of moisture—disputed place with one another in tangled profusion.

There were numerous clearings, for their route lay along a main road. In one hollow, where a creek crossed the road, they passed a turpentine still, and near it a cooper shop, where barrels were made to receive the product of the still. And a little further along they saw between the trees a conical earth-covered mound, the thin column of smoke rising from the top of which revealed a burning tar-kiln. They passed several small cart-loads of pine wood, drawn by mules or stunted oxen, on the way to market. The unenlightened observer would think that so useful a friend as the pine would be treated kindly. But the natives send their women and children out into the woods to cut down the saplings for fire wood.

About two miles out of the town they passed a large plantation, extending back a mile from the road, to judge by the eye. There were wide stretches of cotton and corn, an extensive vineyard, numerous outhouses, and, a few rods back from the road, embosomed in a shady grove, a stately mansion, in the colonial style, with broad, two-storied piazzas running around three sides of it. Before the door stood the carriage which Lowrey had seen drive away from the depot a half-hour before, and on the front piazza sat several of the party who had occupied the carriage.

"Dis yer," said Mr. Pate, "is Kunnel Brewin'ton's place. Kunnel Brewin'ton wuz de riches' man roun' dese parts. He use' ter own mo' slaves 'n any man in de county. But he always treated 'em well, and ev'ybody liked 'im. He owned 'bout half de county, an' dis is de fines' plantation in de neighborhood. Dat young lady what we seed at de depot is Kunnel Brewin'ton's onl daughter, and dis plantation b'longs ter her now. Ole Miss Brewin'ton, e's daid too, and Miss' Ochiltree, Kunnel Brewin'ton's sister an' a widder, she keeps house fer 'im. She's kinder hard an' sharp, an' de colored folks doan lack her much—ner nobody e'se, I reckon. But young Miss Flo'ence, she's de belle. She's be'n 'way ter school most er de time, but w'en she comes back dey has lively times at de plantation—balls an' pahties an' comp'ny all de time. Dey say she doan keer much 'bout it herse'f, but Miss Ochiltree is monst'us fond er comp'ny. Miss Flo'ence is a fine-lookin' gal, and proud as proud kin be. She doan look at common white folks ez much mo' d'n dirt, an' ez fer niggers, dey ain't no mo' ter her d'n dust, er smoke."

Lowrey listened with only an occasional word to show his attention. The cart went round a bend in the road, and having passed an intervening stretch of woodland, they came to another clearing. The fields were planted, but the fences were not in good repair, and the large house, standing back some distance from the road, did not seem well cared for. An air of neglect pervaded the premises.

"Whose place is this?" said Lowrey, with lazy curiosity.

"Dis plantation useter b'long ter olé Miss McIntyre. Miss McIntyre wuz a' ole maid. She owned dis place an' a plantation over de river, an' she lef' it all ter her niece an' neffy young Mistah Bob Utley, an' Miss Flo'ence Brewin'ton, when dey bofe growed up. Dey b'en 'gaged ter be married ever since dey b'en child'en, so de property won't haf ter be 'vided, an' dey say de weddin' is gwine ter come off soon. My wife useter b'long ter Kunnel Brewin'ton, so she knows all 'bout de fam'ly affairs. Wake up dar, Sherman, an' make de san' fly!"

The mule made a great show of speed, and trotted for fully four rods before he relapsed into a walk.

"Young Bob Utley, he lives on dis plantation. A' ole colored woman keeps house fer 'im, but he doan spen' much time at home. Most er de time he's either over ter Kunnel Brewin'ton's, or in town, or ridin' roun' on his black mare, Satan. It's Satan ridin' Satan, ef all tales is true; fer dey say young Mistah Utley is fast as dey make 'em, drinkin', gamblin' an' rakin'. But he's gwine git married dis Fall, dey say, sho', an' w'en Miss Flo'ence git hol' of 'im he'll walk straight, er dey'll be trouble. Go 'long dere, mewil! We won't git home ternight ef you doan pick up dem lazy huffs er yo'n!"

"Are there any people in the settlement by the name of Oxendine?" asked Lowrey carelessly.

"Oxendine? No, dey ain' no Oxendines b'longs roun' yere. Dey's lots er Campbells an' McIntyres and McMillans, and Tho'ntons and Kyles, and plenty yuther names, but dey ain' no Oxendine fambly roun' yere; leas'ways I doan member none."

"There are a good many Oxendines down in Sampson County, where I came from," said the teacher, "and I didn't know but there might be some in this county. It's a common name down there."

"Come ter study, now," said the old man, after a reflective pause, of which Sherman took advantage by again slackening his pace, " 'pears ter me I did heah dere wuz a po' white 'oman wid a likely daughter moved on de sand hills heah lately, ober to'ds de Lumberton plankroad. But I doan know 'em. Dey ain' no rich white folks by dat name, ner no colored folks; po' bockrah doan count. What in de worl' is de matter wid you, mewil? G'long dar, er I'll lam' de hide off'n you!"

The sun was getting down behind the trees, and Lowrey sprang from the cart and walked beside it along a shady stretch of road. A light breeze had sprung up, and as they went down a gentle declivity, the resinous quality of the air mingled with the perfume of the honeysuckle and the smell of running water. Ere they reached the branch at the bottom them passed a wayside spring from which a little negro girl with a yellow gourd was dipping water into a piggin. She looked up with lively curiosity as the cart approached.

"Hoddy, Unker Isaac," she said to the old man, meantime casting sidelong glances at the stranger.

"Hoddy, chile," replied the elder. "How's yo' mammy?"

"She's well. How's all yo' folks?" said the girl, as she deftly lifted the piggin to her bare head.

"Dey all tol'able. Dis is yo' new teacher, chile. Make him yo' bes' bow."

She stood erect, straight as an arrow, with the piggin balanced on her crown, and dropped a low courtesy.

"I hope we shall be better acquainted," said the teacher, with a smile.

Lowrey plucked a spray of honeysuckle that overhung the spring, and breathed its fragrance with long-drawn inhalations.

"Be sho' an' come ter school Monday mawnin, honey," said the old man, as he again touched up the mule with his hickory, "an' tell all de chil'en yer see dat de noo teacher's come."

She stood and watched them until they had crossed the branch at the foot of the hill and ascended the opposite slope. When they reached the top the mule quickened his pace without urging and in a few minutes they arrived at the end of their journey.

Chapter 2

Tom Lowrey had come to Sandy Run to teach the district school for colored children. This was not his only reason for coming, but it was necessary that he should earn his own living, and he could do this best by teaching. So he had sought this school as soon as he had learned that by coming thither he could also further the dearest object of his life.

The day following his arrival was Sunday. Mrs. Pate, a fat and jolly mulatto woman, on whom the maternal cares attendant upon a family of fifteen had borne so lightly that at forty-five she looked ten years younger, prepared in special honor of the guest a breakfast of biscuit and fried chicken, of which he partook in company with Deacon Pate, the children breakfasting in relays, according to their ages, after the men had eaten.

"Chu'ch begins at half past' nine, Brer Lowry," said the deacon, picking his teeth with a jack-knife as they rose from the table. "I reckon a little religion 'll go good on top er dat chicken. 'Pears ter me de Lawd 'ain' done so bad by de cullud folks after all. He made 'em po' an' black, but he give 'em religion an' chickens, de two things dey 'preciates mos'. Understand me," he added, with deference to his visitor's profession, "I doan mean no disrespec' ter book-larnin'. But," he continued, with admirable philosophy, "larnin', aftuh all, is jes' sump'n ter git sump'n e'se wid—a kin' of a hook ter go fishin' wid. It'll he'p you to read de' Bible and to understan' religion mo' an' better, an' it'll he'p you 'arn money fer ter buy chickens wid. Fer de ole style er gittin' chickens is mos' played out in dese days. De school-house an' de chu'ch has made it disgraceful, an' de jail has made it dange'ous. So I stan's by religion, an' chicken and school-houses. Religion fer de soul, chicken fer de body, and larnin' fer ter prokyo' 'em bofe wid."

They went to church at the appointed hour. Lowrey was introduced to a number of the people. He made himself agreeable, invited them to come and see him, and tried to make as favorable an impression on them as he could. They were slightly shy at first of this white young man, who looked and bore himself so little like one of themselves, but his frankness and cordial good-humor soon dissipated this feeling. He was invited to teach a class at Sunday School, and was given a dozen or so of girls, among whom he noticed the little black girl he had met at the spring the day before. He gave her a smile of recognition, and she responded with a pleased display of ivory. When the Sunday School was over Lowrey went home to dinner with the Pates.

There was no afternoon service at Sandy Run Church on this particular Sunday. Lowrey had several things upon his mind, and would have preferred his own thoughts for company. But Deacon Pate was impressed with his own responsibilities as host, and so kept close by his visitor. Lowrey said little, but the deacon could talk enough for two, and so found him a charming companion. The deacon's observations on men and things were shrewd and sometimes witty, but by no means profound enough to be worthy of record.

A little later in the afternoon the people of the settlement began to drop in, so that by four or five o'clock there was quite a number of them gathered under the shade of the China trees in Deacon Pate's yard. Each introduction to a newcomer was after the following formula:

Elder Pate. "Brer Lowrey, 'low me ter make yer 'quainted wid Brer Scott"—or whatever the name might be—"one er de pat'ons ev yo' school. Brer Scott, ou' noo teacher, Brer Lowrey."

Lowrey. "Mr. Scott, I am glad to meet you, and hope we shall be better acquainted."

Brer Scott. "De same ter you, Brer Lowrey. How's all yo' folks?"

In the intervals of Deacon Pate's introductions and Lowrey's explanations that his folks were all well when he last had heard from them, Lowrey received some information about his field of labor, and much advice as to how to conduct a school in order to secure the best results.

"Brer Lowrey," said the preacher, Elder Larkins, who was among the many callers—a tall dark man, with side whiskers, and wearing a badly fitting coat of clerical cut, somewhat the worse for wear, and a linen stock, very much wilted since the morning—"I'se b'en pastah er dis chu'ch fer fo' years, an' I'se seed ez many teachers try ter run de Sandy Run School, an' I knows w'at kind er wuk you got cut out befo' you. W'at you needs mos' is stric'ness. I trus' you will 'member de Scripture injuncture—'Spar' de rod an' spile de chile'. Pray de Lawd ter gib stren'th ter yo' ahm an' nerve ter yo' heart. Ef you needs any he'p, call on me. I use'ter teach school myse'f, an' I kin wiel' de rod er discipline ez well es I kin de swo'd er de Sperrit. Did you hab sump'n ter say, Brer Revels?"

This question was addressed to Mr. Absalom Revels, who by several hems and haws during the preacher's speech had indicated that there was something on his mind. Mr. Revels was a straight-haired yellow man, and this fact, joined to the ownership of a farm in his own right, among a people who were mostly black and as a rule croppers or tenant-farmers, lent him some distinction and gave additional weight to his utterances. Mr. Revels was also the father of half a dozen girls, of ages varying from nine to eighteen.

"I wuz merely goin' ter ast if Mr. Lowrey wuz a married man," he said.

"I'm sorry to say I am not," replied Lowrey, with a light laugh—"sorry for myself, I mean. There is no lady so unfortunate as to be Mrs. Lowrey."

"I dunno 'bout dat," said the preacher. "Dey might go fu'ther an' fare wusser. I *beg* yo' pahdun, Brer Revels, fer interruptin'."

"Ez I wuz erbout ter say," said Mr. Revels, "when de Elder 'sturbed my train er thought, I don't reckon you'll have enny trouble 'bout suitin' yo'se'f in dis settlement. We has gals here dat is young an' good-lookin', and what's mo', we's got gals what'll have lan' some day. Ef yo' ever want young comp'ny, you'll always be welcome at my house, Mr. Lowrey, an' my gals will try ter make it pleasant fer you."

At the approach of evening the visitors departed. Mr. Revels was the last to leave, and Lowrey walked out to the road with him. Just as they reached the bars a young white man rode by on a powerful black horse. He drew rein, nodded carelessly to Mr. Revels, who removed his hat and bowed ceremoniously.

"How's cotton, Revels?" the rider asked.

"Jes' tol'able Mr. Utley, jes tol'able. I doan 'low we're goin' ter have more'n half a crop."

"Come around and see me sometime, Revels; I'd like to talk to you about that sorrel mare of yours."

"Yes, suh, I'll drop in sometime er nuther," replied Revels, as the young man nodded again and rode away.

"He looks like somebody," said Lowrey, watching the easy action of the horse and the graceful seat of the rider, a man of apparently twenty-five years, tall, dark, and strikingly handsome.

"That's young Mistah Bob Utley. You must 'a' passed his place on yo' way f'm town yistiddy. I wonder w'at he's b'en doin' up on the Lumberton plankroad. Up ter some debilment I 'spec'. I'd lack ter sell dat sorrel mare er mine, but I'd lack ter see de money fer 'er, an' Mistah Utley's mighty po' pay."

When Revels had gone Lowrey stood by the bars and looked longingly toward the point of the compass from which Utley had come. That, then, was the way to the Lumberton plankroad. He would very much have liked to take a walk in that direction. But there was not time enough before supper, and he could think of no plausible pretext for taking such a walk at night. He was a patient man, however, for a young man, and could wait, remembering that the race was not to the swift, but to him that held out. He had waited a month, and could wait a little longer. The situation in which he found himself was rather more complicated than he had expected, and too great precipitancy might mar rather than further his plans.

Chapter 3

$\mathcal{O}$n Monday morning, about eight o'clock, Lowrey, escorted by a body-guard of Jefferson Pate's descendants, set out for the scene of his labors during the next two months, the length of the school term provided by law for free public instruction. The school-house, a rude log structure with a clapboarded roof, stood on the ridge of a sand hill, in a little clearing in the pines. With the singular disregard of esthetic considerations or minor physical comforts, characteristic of rural house building, every tree whose shade might have mitigated the summer heat or softened the glare of the sunlight had been cut down, for a distance of fifty or sixty feet on either side of the school-house. The windows of the hut were unglazed, and provided with wooden shutters. There were cracks in the floor, where the unplaned green lumber of which it was laid had shrunk, and the planks rattled under foot when stepped upon. There were cracks in the wall, where the mud that had filled the spaces between the unhewn logs had fallen out. There was a weatherbeaten aspect about this rude temple of learning, in keeping with the character and the fortunes of the community. The law of the State provided for free schools, but public opinion—the opinion of the governing class—still regarded free schools as a burden upon a community not yet recovered from the impoverishment and industrial paralysis resulting from the Civil War; the result of these conflicting forces was that Sandy Run School had a two-months term, in the school-house just described.

There was quite a gathering of children, some sitting in the school-house, some standing in groups, and others reclining on the ground in the edge of the forest. The teacher had heard them laughing and talking as he drew near, but when he turned into the clearing from the road, a silence as of the grave fell over them. But Lowrey felt that every eye was upon him, and that during the day, his every word and movement would be observed and commented upon. He was young enough to be self-conscious and rather uncomfortable under this battery of unfamiliar eyes.

Going into the school-house, he gave a smiling "Good-morning" to the half-dozen older girls who had taken their seats inside. Some of them nodded, one snickered audibly, and almost strangled herself trying to cover the breach of decorum with a cough; and several others responded with a "Good mornin'" so timid that one would have thought them afraid of the sound of their own voices.

Lowrey took out of his pocket a small hand-bell and set it on the rude board, placed across two uprights, which served as a desk. He then opened the blank book he had brought for a register and made the following entry on the fly leaf:

> Sandy Run Colored School,
> Thomas H. Lowrey, Teacher.
> Term began, Aug. 3, 188_.

As it was not yet quite time to open school, he next looked around for some one from whom to seek information. He was about to call up one of the older girls, when his eyes rested on a face he had seen before. It was that of the little black girl he had met at the spring on Saturday. She was neatly dressed in a clean homespun frock, her hair elaborately "corn-rowed," and sat just a short distance from the teacher, her black, bead-like eyes fixed intently upon him with an expression of mingled curiosity and admiration. He beckoned her and she sprang to the desk. As she stood before him he was struck by the contrast between the old and wizened look of her ugly little face, with its gleaming eyes, and the meager childish figure surmounted by it. She might have been a precocious child of ten or an older girl of stunted growth. This latter supposition was strengthened by the attitude in which she stood, with her shoulders thrown back at such an angle as to suggest a malformation of the spine.

"What is your name?" he asked.

"Mississippi Nova Scotia Rose Amelia Sunday."

She delivered this incongruous string of names in a rapid monotone so droll that it required an effort on Lowrey's part to repress a smile.

"Say it over again," he said gravely, "and say it slowly, so that I can take it all in."

She repeated her name.

"Is that all?"

"Dat's all, suh. I had some mo', but t'other teacher said dat was all he could git on one line in de roll-book; so I done forgot de res'. "

"And what do they call you at home?"

"Dey calls me 'Shug.' "

"Short for 'Sugar.' Well, I'll call you Rose Amelia."

"Yes, suh. 'Rose 'Melia Sunday'—is dat w'at my name gwine be?"

"Yes, I'll write it—'Rose Amelia Sunday.' What time did your last teacher open school in the morning, Rose Amelia?"

"Oh, he 'menced school mos' any time; gin'ally 'bout six or half-pas'. I didn't knowed w'at time you wuz gwine begin dis mawnin'. We uns is b'en here, mos' un us, sence sun-up."

"And what time did the other teacher dismiss school?"

"You mean let school out?"

"Yes."

"W'en it got too dahk fer ter read. Is you a *rale* black man?" she asked inconsequentially, with sudden daring.

"Not *real* black. I was left out in the rain an' got some of it washed off. But I'm black enough to teach you."

She stared at him a moment, and then grinned appreciatively.

Lowrey asked Rose Amelia a few questions about the books used, and the classification and methods of instruction employed by his predecessor in office, but neither from Rose Amelia nor another intelligent looking girl whom he called up, to her very evident embarrassment, could he learn of anything he considered worthy of adoption.

At nine o'clock he rang the bell, which brought the rest of the pupils flocking in. The larger ones took the back seats. The little ones all tried at first to crowd on the same seat, but failing, attempted each to get a separate bench, in which they were equally unsuccessful, as there were not benches enough to go around.

"Those on the front seat," said the teacher, "will come forward and give their names. The girl on the left first."

She came forward, a tall light-brown girl, dressed in blue calico, with a bright red ribbon around her throat by way of ornament.

"Your name, please?"

"Louisa Revels." Lowrey entered the name in his register, and thought as he looked at her that Mr. Revels' wife must be darker than her husband. It was a very natural thought, for questions of color are of paramount importance in the Southern States.

"What have you studied, Louisa?"

"I've studied the spellin'-book. I've b'en clean over to 'incomprehensibility' "—which, it may be stated for the benefit of those who do not know, is one of a list of polysyllables contained in the last pages of Websters' blue-backed spelling-book, the palladium of Southern education since the days of Noah Webster.

Lowrey took the spelling-book she handed him, and opened it at random.

"Read that page."

She read, or rather recited it, with great fluency in an expressionless monotone.

"Can you write?"

"Yes, sir."

Lowrey handed her a pencil. She wrote her name, an awkward scrawl, but legible. The teacher made a note of Louisa's qualifications and then called up the next girl. This one could read but could not write. The next could only spell as far as "baker," another intellectual landmark in the spelling-book. The next could spell wonderfully, in a parrot-like way, with no comprehension of the meaning of the words, and could not read at all. Another had an old arithmetic and could say the multiplication table as far as the sixes, but could not get beyond "six times seven," while another brought with her a geography in which Poland was set down as an independent sovereignty and the Great American Desert represented as extending over the western half of the continent.

When the girls had been enrolled and examined, the teacher called up one of the boys, a very dark youth of probably fifteen years.

"What is your name?"

"J. M. Golightly, suh."

"What does the 'J' stand for?"

"Jere', suh."

"And the 'M'?"

"Miah, suh. Mah whole name is Jeremiah Golightly."

"Can you read, Jere?"

"Yas, suh," with promptness and confidence.

Lowrey opened an elementary geography at a simple descriptive passage.

"I cain't read that," said Jere hastily; "I never l'arned ter read that. I can read the spellin'-book."

"But you can surely read that, if you can read anything."

But Jere could not read it. He knew the words as troubles come—by battalions, but not by single spies—as babies know the rhymes of Mother Goose.

It was now half-past ten and Lowrey dismissed his school for a brief recess. When he called them in again he completed the examination, and on summing it up, found that only two or three pupils could read simple English taken at random, though most had learned some part of the spelling-book by rote. Of useful knowledge they were grossly ignorant. Sandy Run School was almost virgin soil. Lowrey divided them into temporary classes, and laid out their lessons, and the room was soon filled with the subdued murmur of whispered words. They all studied with their lips, a habit which the teacher meant to break them of.

At twelve o'clock school was dismissed for an hour. The children dispersed throughout the clearing, and in the woods and along the road. Most of them turned toward the spring, half way down the hill behind the school-house. Their bashfulness had worn off somewhat during the morning, and Lowrey could hear them talking and laughing together. He ate his lunch in the schoolroom, and then putting on his hat, walked down to the spring. Rose Amelia was sitting on a fallen log near the spring with an open spelling-book before her, apparently deeply immersed in study. She dropped the book as the teacher drew near and sprang to hand him a drink of water from the gourd that hung by the spring.

"Thank you, Rose Amelia."

He replaced the gourd and walked back up the hill. About midway the ascent, in a shaded spot he flung himself on the ground and leaned his shoulder against the trunk of a tall pine. Rose Amelia followed him up the hill, and stood, with her hands folded behind her, looking at the teacher with an air of respectful familiarity.

"Well, Rose Amelia, have you eaten your lunch?"

"Yas, suh, I had a 'tater an' a piece er bread. Daddy says yer kain' l'arn ef yer eats too much. Did yer bring yo' own dinner?"

"Yes."

"To'ther teacher always had his'n brung to him—used 'ter sen' one er de scholars ter fetch it. I used ter go an' git his dinner. Would yer lack ter hab me bring yo'n?"

"No," he said, "I hardly think it necessary. It would take you away from your books too long."

She seemed disappointed, but soon brightened up.

"How many hick'ries a day is yer gwine ter use?" she asked.

"Oh, I don't know. I haven't figured out how many I shall need."

"T'other teacher used a dozen hick'ries a day. I sh'd think that 'ud be ernuff."

"I don't know about that," Lowrey answered with judicial gravity. "Whether a dozen will be sufficient or not depends on how things go, I can tell you. And besides, the quality of the hickories is a matter for consideration in determining the number."

Rose Amelia beamed with satisfaction. "Kin I git yo' hick'ries?" she asked eagerly. "I knows whar dey's splendid hick'ries. T'other teacher alluz let me git his'n."

"And then let you escape whipping?"

"No, suhree!" she said, drawing herself up proudly, "I useter git mo' lammin's 'n any gal in school, 'ca'se I couldn' l'arn ter spell good. Daddy says a teacher w'at don't whip ain't wuth shucks. Daddy thought a heap er t'other teacher."

"Your father is a man of decided opinions," said the teacher, stretching himself.

"Oh, yes, my daddy is a smaht man. He dips tuppentine in Summer an' hauls wood in Winter—when he's home."

"Is he at home now?"

"No," she said with some embarrassment, "he had some bad luck, an' had ter go 'way fer a while. But we 'spec's him back in erbout fo' weeks."

When the hour was ended the teacher called his school together, and resumed the task of bringing order out of intellectual chaos. By the time for dismissal he had made hopeful progress; and he felt that he could reasonably anticipate a successful school term; and as he had both zeal for learning and an honest desire to benefit the children under his charge, this feeling lent him pleasure and encouragement.

Emerging from the school-house, he found Rose Amelia Sunday waiting at the door, and she walked by his side for a good part of his way homeward.

"Rose Amelia," he asked, "where is the white school?"

"The white school is kep' in Snow Hill Baptis' Chu'ch," she said, " 'bout two mile from yere, on de Lumberton Plankroad."

She pointed out to him, as they passed it, the road which, leaving their own road at an angle, led into the Lumberton Road beyond. He noted the place, and looked longingly in that direction. But Rose Amelia kept along with him, and others of his pupils were only a little in advance of them, and a straggling group of boys was no great distance behind. So he went on his way, and spent the rest of the day at his boarding-place.

Chapter 4

*I*t was several days before the teacher found an opportunity to take the wished-for walk over to the Lumberton Road. The Pate children, for the first few days, until the novelty wore off, accompanied him to school in the morning. And when they were not with him, Rose Amelia was. This queer, elfish person attached herself to Lowrey, and followed him around in a manner which he attempted to discourage, but without much success. She would lay in wait for him on the way to school, and join him at the intersection of her own homeward road with the road he came. She would hover about him at recess, waiting patiently for him to notice her, talking freely, with the slightest encouragement, about the people she knew, and displaying in her remarks a shrewdness and wisdom beyond her apparent years, coupled with a frankness that was at times quite amusing.

By the end of the week Lowrey had got his school well in hand, and his impatience had increased to such an extent that he could no longer defer the enterprise to which he had been looking forward since he came to Sandy Run, and which indeed had been the prime motive of his coming.

On Friday afternoon he dismissed his school somewhat earlier than usual. He had learned that the white school at Snow Hill let out at five o'clock, and he let his pupils go at half-past four, thus giving himself a half-hour to make the distance necessary to reach the Lumberton Plankroad.

Rose Amelia loitered behind the other children, and he saw her waiting at the door.

"Rose Amelia," he said, "don't wait for me. I'm not going yet, and when I do leave I'm not going directly home. I'll see you at Sunday School day after to-morrow," he added, seeing her air of disappointment.

She went away slowly, and with many a lingering backward look.

Lowrey watched her from a crack in the log wall of the school-house, until she had disappeared behind the first bend in the road, and then locking the door he set out in the same direction. He could hear now and then a faint sound of laughter, or an echoing halloa, from some of his pupils who were ahead of him, and for a time he went cautiously, for he did not want company, nor did he wish to attract attention to his movements. When he reached the road leading to the plankroad, he turned into it and breaking into a run, with brief slackenings of his speed for breath, quickly covered the mile that separated him from the plankroad. He stationed himself in the underbrush at the point where the roads met, and in such a position that he could command a view of the plankroad for nearly a quarter of a mile toward Snow Hill school-house, and yet remain concealed from sight.

He then looked at his watch; it was just five o'clock. He waited fifteen minutes. A white woman came by with a basket on her arm. An old negro drove past with an ox-cart; and a heavy wagon drawn by four mules, on the way to the neighboring cotton mill, ploughed its way through the white sand of the road-way. For the planks in the road had long since rotted, and the highway was a plankroad in name only. But no school children appeared, and Lowrey began to grow anxious. He thought perhaps he had been misinformed as to the hour of dismission, or that the teacher, like himself, had for some reason departed from the rule. It seemed as though he had been waiting an hour, and he was beginning to fear his waiting was in vain, when suddenly in the distance the shouts of escaped school children rang through the air. In five minutes a number of them passed by where he was hidden. One of them came near his hiding-place, but did not see him. When they had gone by he waited five minutes longer, his impatience increasing with the minutes in geometrical progression. He had almost reached the conclusion that his errand was in vain, for this day at least, when he caught sight of a slender figure in sunbonnet and calico gown, spelling-book in hand, coming slowly down the road from the direction of the school-house.

His heart gave a great bound, and it was with an effort that he restrained his eagerness and waited quietly until she drew near, when he came forward, as though he had just come up the intersecting road, and met her face to face.

As Mandy Oxendine, for it was she, approached, she seemed preoccupied. But whatever her thoughts were, they underwent a change when she looked up, and saw the figure confronting her; and it would not be saying too much to say that she was startled, as she might easily be, at meeting so unexpectedly, in such an unlikely place, one who was not at all in her thoughts, and whom she had every reason to believe a hundred miles away. The expression of her face, whose swiftly changing play revealed her thoughts, when the first shock of the meeting was over, denoted in turn, recognition, surprise, and a shade of apprehension. Lowrey, who was reading her countenance, looked searchingly, but in vain, for any token of pleasure therein. There was no sign of repugnance; her expression was certainly not one of indifference; but if there was any kindlier feeling, it was overshadowed for the time being by other and more insistent emotions. She looked up the road, and then turning, cast a rapid glance behind her, and, seemingly relieved at seeing no one in sight, turned and faced the young man.

"How d'ye do, Mandy," he said, extending his hand.

"I don't know why I should shake hands with you, Tom Lowrey. Shakin' han's is a sign of frien'ship," she answered, in a voice every tone of which sent a thrill to his heart. The mere sight of her had filled him with a warm glow of pleasure, and for a moment he wondered how he had lived so near her through the last week without seeing her.

"Ain't I your friend, Mandy?" he asked, still keeping his hand extended.

"You ought to know. *I* reckon not."

"You know I am, and more than your friend—your own true lover."

"Actions speak louder than words. You said that once before an' yet you went away an' lef' me, and stayed away two years."

"You know why I went away," he said, "and that it was for your sake I went. I wanted to learn something so I could be somebody, and give you a chance."

"Yes," she said, "an' you lef' me in the woods, 'mongs' niggers, and tu'pentine trees, an' snakes an' screech-owls. An' I got tired of 'em."

"When I came back," he went on, not heeding her interruption, "you were gone. It took me a week to find out where you had gone, and when I did I came here."

"And now that you've come here, you may go away," she said. "When I wanted you, you wuzn't there; an' now I don't want you, you've turned up. Ef you are a friend of mine, yo'll go away and stay away. You lef' me 'mongs' niggers, an' I wouldn' be a nigger, fer God made me white," she added passionately, "an' I 'termined ter be what God made me, an' I *am* white. Nobody here knows anything different, an' nobody will, unless you come here with your frien'ship and tell it."

She looked superb as she stood with an angry flush on her cheeks and an angry glitter in her eyes, declaring her independence, her revolt against iron custom. In her intensity of feeling she had drawn herself up to her full height, and the statuesque lines of a noble figure, unspoiled by the distorting devices of fashion, were visible through a frock whose scantness lent but little envious drapery to conceal them. Her gingham sunbonnet had fallen back, disclosing a luxuriant head of nut-brown hair, with varying tints and golden gleams as the light fell on it at different angles. By intuition or inspiration, she had gathered it into a Greek knot, which brought out the contour of a head, small but perfectly proportioned. Her eyes were gray, but looked almost black as they reflected her emotion.

"But that needn't keep you from being my friend," he said. "You are no whiter than you used to be. You are taller, though," he said as he looked her over admiringly, "and prettier, and prouder. But all *that* needn't hinder you from being my friend."

"That depen's on mo' than one thing. What are you doin' here? Did you jes' foller me," she said, with the calm air of sovereignty with which a beautiful woman assumes that it is a small matter for any man to follow her to the ends of the earth, "or are you workin' at somethin'?"

"I'm teaching the Sandy Run colored school."

Mandy at this statement looked up and down the road again. "Then you can't be my frien'," she said decisively. "A person has got to be white or black in this worl', an' I ain't goin' to be black. An' black folks an' white folks don't go together. Ef you should be seen with me, it wouldn' do you no good, for folks know you as colored, an' it would ruin me. I'd ruther die than to be a nigger again," she said, fiercely, "to be hated by black folks because I'm too white, and despised by white folks because I'm not white enough."

"You talk," said Lowrey, with a tinge of sadness, "as though God didn't make black people."

"He made 'em; an' he made 'em black, an' ugly an' pore."

"That doesn't sound well from your lips," he said reproachfully.

"But come with me, and I will take you away, far away, and we will both be white. It was for you that I went away to get learning, and for you I'd be white or black—or blue or green, if it would please you, sweetheart," he said, as he seized her hand, which was hanging by her side.

She drew back slightly, as he advanced toward her, but she made no very great effort to withdraw her hand.

"I'll finish out my school," he said, "and I'll take the money, and we'll go away, and I'll work and study; and having a white man's chance, I'll make money, and you shall be a white lady."

He drew still nearer, and passed his arm around her waist. His lips were approaching hers, when she pulled herself away.

"No," she said, "you're too late. When you might have had me you wouldn't take me, an' now I am goin' to marry another man."

Lowrey turned pale, and trembled as though he had been shot.

"May I ask," he said hoarsely, after the first shock of the announcement, "who is the happy man?"

"He's a gentleman," she said, more softly, as she perceived his evident distress. "You say you're my frien'. Ef you are, I should think you'd like to see me do well. He is a gentleman; he is white, he is rich, he rides on horseback, he lives in a big house."

"Who is he?" said Lowrey, with dull anger.

"I won't tell you," she said.

"You shall tell me," he replied fiercely. "Who is this fine gentleman that will marry a sand-hill mulatto?"

"You forgit," she retorted, "I'm passin' for white—"

"Who is this fine man on horseback who will marry a sand-hill poor-white girl?"

"I shan't tell you. He says he will marry me, and he will make a lady of me, now, without waiting till I'm old an' gray."

"He *says* he will marry me," sneered the young man, mimicking her tone, "and he *says* he will make a lady of me. How long have you known this man?"

"I don't like the way you talk to me," she said petulantly. "You speak as if I belonged to you or you had some right over me."

"I have the right every man has to protect a woman against a scoundrel."

"You've taken your own time to assert your right. I've known him three weeks."

"He *says* he will marry you and make a fine lady of you. And what do his folks say about it?"

"I don't know them—yet. It's a secret yet."

"They say pretty women are all fools," he said, despondently, "and you are the biggest fool of them all. He *says* he will marry you. Perhaps—he ought to have married you already!" he cried, as a hateful thought struck him. He glared at Mandy as though he would read her heart.

She had shrunk for a moment before his anger, but at this insinuation a quick flush of offended maidenhood suffused her face and throat.

"You ought to know me well enough, Tom Lowrey," she retorted spiritedly, "to know that I am an honest gal, whatever my faults may be. Tom Lowrey, you are no friend o' mine. I'm goin'."

She walked proudly away, and did not deign to look back.

"Good-by, Mandy—" contritely. "I'm sorry I said it."

She did not reply, but kept steadily on her way. He stood watching her, and started once to follow her, but after taking several steps he changed his mind, and, waiting until she had passed out of sight, returned home by the road he had come.

Chapter 5

$\mathcal{T}$om Lowrey and Mandy Oxendine, or, more correctly speaking, Amanda Oxendine, had been brought up in a small town about seventy-five miles from Sandy Run. They were descendants of free colored people, a class which in North Carolina was numerically stronger before the war than in any State of the Union. While the deadly blight of slavery paralyzed the energies of North Carolina, along with those of her sister Southern States, it did not seem at that time to dry up the milk of human kindness in her breast, and even to her black children she gave some small measure of opportunity, and some small share of comfort and happiness. The free colored people had schools; they held property; some of them—a curious fact—were themselves slaveholders. They constituted almost entirely the mechanics and skilled artisans of the State. Up to 1845, when the Nat Turner insurrection in Virginia made slavery for a moment tremble, they possessed the right of suffrage, and exercised it at the polls. When the development of the cotton industry consequent upon the invention of the cotton-gin gave slavery a fresh impetus, the free colored people, in common with all their mother-race, felt the growing weight of oppression; they lost their suffrage, and henceforth they merely lived by sufferance, for under the theory of slavery there was no place for them in the community. But even under these unfavorable conditions the relatively friendly and harmonious relations in which they had lived with their white neighbors in certain parts of the State were not entirely destroyed.

These free people of color were often more white than black, and in many of them a constant infusion of white blood had almost wiped out the darker strain. Some of them had taken their origin from the Tuscarora and Cherokee tribes, once numerous in North Carolina. The Indian women in former generations had mated with negro men, with whom they were more nearly on a social level than with the whites. The stock thus originated, supplemented by manumitted slaves, and by runaways from contiguous provinces, with a liberal infusion of white blood, had in the course of time developed into the free colored people or "old issue" free negroes of North Carolina. Despised and of no account socially among white people, they in turn looked down upon the slaves, and thus constituted a class apart, forming more nearly a parallel to the mulattoes in the French West Indies than to any other social caste of the Western world.

If there is anything in the supposed mysterious affinities of race, it is not strange that among these people, thus unequally fused of diverse elements in the alembic of nature, there should be many instances in which the preponderating blood of the individual should seek its own. If the tendency were downward toward the black substratum there was no obstruction to it. But any attempted upward movement on the part of those who were nearly white, was met by the iron barrier of caste, to overleap which involved a severance from one's former life almost as complete as that made by death; one must forsake home and relatives and friends, must cease to see them, to communicate with them, to inquire of them. It was a heroic remedy, and demanded either great courage or great meanness, according to the point of view.

But Mandy Oxendine had taken this step. There was no external evidence of negro blood in Mandy, unless a slight softening of facial outline, a dreaminess of eye, a mellowness of accent, might have been ascribed to its presence. Added to these she had a feminine charm all her own, a grace of movement, a perfection of form, bestowed by nature in a generous mood, not perceptibly affected by either ignorance or poverty or rude surroundings. The best man is but ore, to be crushed and ground and smelted to get at what is in him. A comely and gracious woman is a nugget of pure gold.

To the beauty nature had given Mandy, the companionship of the somber pines had imparted a tinge of sadness; the calm and solitude of country life had superinduced repose. And the blood of three races commingled had resulted in a complexity of temperament very uncommon in the sand-hill people of North Carolina. She was ambitious. She was black in theory; therefore she would be white—as the poor would be rich or the sick would be well. To be white meant opportunity, and to him who has it not, opportunity means everything—once attained, its value is problematical. She had persuaded her mother to move away from their native county in furtherance of her plan, and for reasons which are no part of this story they had come to the neighborhood of Sandy Run. They had left no near kindred behind to mourn their departure or to be hurt by their desertion. They were entire strangers in Sandy Run "settlement," and the distance of seventy-five miles from their former home was a barrier as wide as the ocean between their past and their present life; for there was no railroad and no well established line of travel between the two places. In the ordinary course of events they might have lived and died on the sandhills at Sandy Run without meeting a former acquaintance.

The appearance of Tom Lowrey, though unlooked for, and contrary to reasonable expectation, was not accidental. Born of the same class, and about as far removed from the black ancestral source, his was a simpler mind, and of stronger fibre. He had grown up to the age of ten or twelve in the atmosphere of intellectual stagnation that prevailed among the poor of his State until war had stirred society to its depths. The new era of hope and opportunity opened by the success of the federal arms had quickened even his childish pulses. He attended a Freedman's Bureau school, and by rare good fortune came under the influence of a noble teacher, who taught for love of humanity and love of God, and who recognized in the lad an instrument for noble ends. Under her guidance his mental horizon broadened, and his ambition grew apace. When his good teacher, succumbing at last to a fatal disease, had gone back to her Northern home, to die among her people, the love of learning she had implanted in the boy, fed by such books as he could find, grew into a burning desire for a better education, a broader culture, and a higher life.

But the years which had brought these longings had also brought adolescence, and Mandy, and love. She had grown up from infancy almost under his eyes, and absorbed in his dreams he had scarcely noticed her. One day, when she was a young woman, he saw the glint of the sunlight on her hair, and loved her. He cherished his love for a while as a precious secret and then told her of it, and she did not repulse him. But while Tom loved Mandy, he did not give up his ambitions.

When he told her of them she was at first uninterested, and afterwards troubled, for young love is jealous of ambitions; a loving woman beloved would be all the world to her lover. When he would dwell upon the point that with learning he could gain wealth and position for her, she listened with more attention. But when he spoke of going away to school for a year she trembled, turned pale, and burst into tears.

"Don't go an' leave me, Tom. I shall never see you again," she sobbed.

"The year will fly, my darlin'," he said, "and be over before you know it. I'll write to you every week."

He kissed her tears away and finally with many forebodings she consented to his departure. He had gone away to an institute in a distant part of the State, where Northern philanthropy had provided opportunity for the higher education of colored youth. There the gates of a new world were unlocked for him. He learned of great nations that had lived and died, of great civilizations that had flourished and decayed, of great philosophies and great religious systems that had been swept away by advancing knowledge as fogs obscuring the light of truth; of great literatures, that had flowered and faded, and perished, leaving only a few of their choicest blossoms, to be forever the delight and the inspiration and the despair of mankind. With the eye of a rare imagination he saw enough of life through the door which learning opened, to realize how little an individual could accomplish compared with the achievements of the race, and to give him, in a degree commensurate with his acquirements, the humility of the philosopher, rather than the arrogance of the scholar. It remained for later years to teach him the value of the individual life, the majesty of the soul.

In the intoxication of learning, for that is the only term fit to express his mental attitude at this time, the image of Mandy was temporarily crowded into the background. There is seldom room in one mind for two great passions. It is true he wrote to her, and for a while regularly. At first he sent a letter once a week, but as Mandy was a poor correspondent, and replied but seldom, his letters fell off to once in two weeks, and from that to once a month; and finally he wrote only when she had answered.

At the end of the first year he was offered a school in the neighborhood of his college. To take it involved the necessity of remaining away from home during the entire vacation. He still loved Mandy, but the offer was a good one, and his teachers advised him to accept it. It was necessary for him to earn money, for he was too proud to owe his living to charity. He wrote to Mandy, explaining the situation, and postponing his return for another year.

When the buggy had driven up to Tom's gate to take him away to school Mandy had been there with his relations and friends to bid him goodbye. He had kissed Mandy, as he had the other women, and she had received the caress with a forced smile; and when he put his arm around her, her heart gave a bound, and she felt an almost uncontrollable impulse to clasp him and hold him and never let him leave her. But by an effort she restrained herself until the last word was said, and Tom, waving his hand in adieu, had disappeared around the first bend in the road. Then she had given way, and rushing into the forest, whose sombre, sighing loneliness was in sympathy with her mood, she had thrown herself prone upon the ground and given way to grief. She divined the effects of distance and absence, and wept for a lover lost.

To her inexperience a year seemed like eternity. So many things might happen—he might be sick, and she could not visit him, he might die without telling her goodby; or most dreadful thought of all, he might forget her and love another. If anyone had predicted that in two years she would be engaged to marry another man she would have repelled the suggestion indignantly, and would have avowed her love to be as lasting as it was obviously single and passionate. She hoped, but she did not expect to see him again. She answered his letters as best she could. This was her reply to his first:

Dear Tom:
I take my pen in han' to let you no that I am well an doin well an hope this will fine you the same. I got yor letter out of the postoffis yistiddy, and was glad to hear that you was well an doin well. It is so lonesome sence you went away. Make 'ase' an git thru school an come back to your own true love.

Mandy.

This missive was written on a half sheet of foolscap beginning close to the top and occupying about one-fourth of the page. The writing was legible, but evidently done with much labor, and one or two blots betrayed an unpracticed hand. Below the signature was rudely traced in ink the figure of a heart, with a fancy scalloped border, and below that, as by an afterthought, this beautiful and brilliant couplet:

> If you love me like I love you,
> No nife can kutt our love in 2.

At first Tom's letters were but little better written, though he found it easier to put his thoughts in words. But as his handwriting improved and his letters were better expressed, she felt the difference, and was ashamed to have him see her poor scrawls. When the year was up and he did not return, her fears were confirmed. She reasoned that if at the end of one year his love was not strong enough to draw him to her it would be less at the end of two years. She did not write to him again.

But the ideas he had planted in her mind did not die. He had talked to her of learning, and of wealth, and of opportunity. Things which she had looked at from afar, as Dives looked at Lazarus in Abraham's bosom, and which she had never thought of except as the inheritance of the white, he had spoken of as attainable by himself and by her. And when she reached the conclusion that he would never return to take her out of the narrow, sordid sphere in which she lived, she determined to seek for herself a new life elsewhere. She had grasped by intuition the essential element of difference in the status of the two races she stood between; she felt that it was not learning or wealth, or even aspiration—but opportunity. And she saw that to have opportunity was to possess the road to all else in life. And so by becoming white she had stepped across the line of demarcation and into the freedom and light of opportunity. She still loved Tom Lowrey, but it was the Tom Lowrey she had known, and she did not know how she would like the new Tom Lowrey, if indeed she should ever see him again. If he came back, and wanted her, he could seek her; indeed it would but serve him right to have to do so. How she would act if he found her, would depend upon circumstances.

At the end of his second year at school Lowrey went home. And as he neared his native town his old love returned with all its former fervor. When he learned that Mandy and her mother had gone, no one knew whither, his love grew ten times stronger than ever. He did not rest until he had traced Mandy to Lafayette County and to the neighborhood of Sandy Run. It was still necessary for him to earn money in order to live, so he had sought for and obtained the appointment as teacher of the Sandy Run colored school.

When he first came it had been his intention to seek out Mandy and try to renew their old relations. He realized that some effort would perhaps be necessary, for he had not acted the part of an ardent lover for two years, and Mandy was a high-spirited girl. But the discovery that she attended the white school and was known as a white girl had put a new aspect upon the situation. He could not visit or converse with her openly; for in his conspicuous position as teacher any intimacy or even acquaintance with her would have attracted remark, would have required explanation, would have endangered Mandy's new and precarious social standing. It was necessary to see her first alone, and find out just where he stood in her regard. If she had received him on the old footing, the way would have been to some extent clear; he could have met her in secret until his school term was over, and then they could have gone away together, and there would have been no scandal and no disturbance of the social life of Sandy Run. But even this difficulty had dwindled into insignificance when he learned of the other lover. The sight of his old sweetheart, whose girlish grace had ripened into a rare womanly beauty, had intensified his passion. He knew enough of the world to realize that this mysterious lover on horseback was a dangerous rival; and he knew enough to fear that he not only stood in imminent danger of losing Mandy, but that she was in serious danger herself. Love, jealousy, fear, and anger, were his bedfellows during the well-nigh sleepless night that followed his first meeting with Mandy on the Lumberton Plankroad.

Chapter 6

*M*ore than a week elapsed before Lowrey saw Mandy again. In the meantime he had got his school well organized, and moving along smoothly and successfully. He had some mischievous pupils, but no examples of obstinacy or open rebellion. The slight infractions of his rules he reproved with a sharp word, and occasionally punished with an added task or a short detention at recess or after school hours. He did not consider it necessary to pound wisdom into the heads of his pupils, or to stimulate their minds by sympathy with their backs, but by patience and kindness sought to direct their untaught feet along the untried path of learning. Rose Amelia was somewhat concerned at the teacher's method of discipline. She came to him at recess one day and said:

"Teacher, ain't it 'bout time I wuz bringin' yer some hick'ries?"

"Well, Rose Amelia, I reckon you'd better get me some. You can cut them after school this evening, and fetch them when you come tomorrow. Be sure and get them long and strong and limber, and with plenty of knots."

"Yes, suh, I'll git 'em; I knows a tree w'ats got jes' dat kin'."

Rose Amelia's eyes danced with an unholy light, and a delicious shiver ran up and down her spine as she heard in imagination the sharp swish of the hickories. Before lessons were resumed after the noon recess she had informed the whole school of her commission, and of the zeal and conscientiousness with which she meant to execute it.

All through the afternoon the teacher felt the eyes of the pupils fixed upon him with renewed interest. There were evidently depths of his character which they had not fathomed nor even suspected. Their last teacher had been a strict disciplinarian, and had not spared the rod. Lowrey's conduct had puzzled them a little, but they had not expected him to teach without whipping. They had looked forward to the time when he should become more severe. But Rose Amelia's statements had invested him with a bloodthirsty ferocity that promised to make their school life extremely interesting.

The next morning Rose Amelia brought a bundle of hickories which would have delighted the heart and satisfied the judgment of a Nero, or a Caligula, or a flagellant of the Middle Ages. Long, strong, supple and knotty, they would have served as admirable substitutes for the knout or cat-o'-nine-tails.

"I reckon them'll do," she said exultingly, as she laid them on the teacher's desk, and stood waiting his acknowledgements.

"Excellently, Rose Amelia. I could never have selected them so well myself. I'm very much obliged to you, and will make good use of them."

Rose Amelia strutted around the schoolyard like a Lord High Executioner. Before the bell rang for the opening of the school, the teacher hung the bundle of rods on a couple of wooden pegs in the wall, where they were in plain sight, a terror to evil-doers. The behavior of the pupils during the morning was perfect. No sound of whispering was heard, no pin was stuck, no rule broken, for several hours, until one small boy, moved by some rash impulse, tempted fate and rushed headlong into danger by whistling aloud.

It was a dreadful moment. A thrill of horrible anticipation ran through the school. The criminal himself perceived too late the enormity of his offence and turned pale—or ashen—with apprehension. Every eye was fixed alternately on the teacher and on Ab'um Linkum, and a pin might have been heard not only to drop but to ring and re-echo through the intense silence.

"Abraham Lincoln Gainey, come forward."

Like the murderer to his fate Ab'um Linkum left his seat, and with widely-distended eyes shambled up in front of the desk.

"Abraham, take down that bundle of hickories."

Abraham, thus condemned to partial hari-kari, stuck his fingers in one crack of the wall, his toes in another and reaching upward his trembling hand seized the bundle of hickories, but could not hold it. The bundle slipped and came down on his head, the fastenings burst, and a shower of switches fell over Abraham and to the floor with a tremendous clatter.

"Now," said the teacher, when Ab'um had picked them up, "find the largest, and strongest and knottiest one, and bring it here."

It required true heroism to execute this order, and Ab'um obeyed it indifferently well.

"Now," said the teacher, "come here, sir."

He led his trembling victim into a corner of the room. Rose Amelia's face beamed with joyful anticipation; her excitement was so great she could scarcely keep her seat.

"Now, open your mouth," said Lowrey, "and hold this hickory in it for fifteen minutes."

That was all the use the teacher ever made of the switches. The fate of Ab'um Linkum inspired such a wholesome fear that he did not have occasion to use them again. There was not a pupil in the school who would not rather have been whipped twice than to hold a switch in his mouth for fifteen minutes.

Rose Amelia, however, was somewhat disappointed, for she was naturally conservative, and did not approve of innovations. But any feeling she had about the switches soon wore away, or was rather swallowed up by the absorbing passion she conceived for Lowrey. She was but a child. To a child's love she added an intensity of feeling, a fervor of devotion, and a jealousy, like those of a mature woman of strong passions. She haunted his footsteps. A smile made her happy, a frown plunged her into deepest gloom of spirit. She almost overworked her poor brain in the effort to win the teacher's commendation. She was mischievous as a monkey, and had a strong spice of malice in her disposition; but she suppressed her bad inclinations, and made herself a model of deportment, for the sake of the teacher's approving smile. She brought him apples, and scuppernong grapes, at the expense of some one's orchard or vineyard on the road to the schoolhouse. She brought him persimmons, and maypops, and chinquapins, and other native delicacies for which she scoured the woods and old fields. She watched for him on the way to school in the morning, hung around him at recess, and waited for him to leave the school-house at night. Lowrey was much preoccupied, and paid but little attention to her. He took her presents, and sometimes asked her to share his lunch, and listened with occasional interest or amusement to her gossip and opinions concerning the people of the settlement. She knew the family history of all the colored folks and many of the white, for a mile or two around, and had their sins and vices carefully catalogued and filed away in her memory for ready reference.

But Lowrey found Rose Amelia's attendance a serious annoyance when he wanted to go up to the Lumberton Plankroad with the hope of meeting Mandy. He did not wish his movements known. He could not often dismiss his school before five o'clock, the usual hour, and if he waited until Rose Amelia and he parted company on their homeward way, it would be too late to intercept Mandy on her way from school. Several times during the week following their first meeting he had run himself out of breath, but had only succeeded once in seeing Mandy pass in company with another girl. On this occasion, as the two girls drew near he stepped out into the road, met and passed them, going in the opposite direction to theirs. He looked at Mandy, but did not venture to speak, and she gave no sign of recognition.

"Oh, Mandy," said her companion, when Lowrey was out of hearing, "who you reckon that is? It's the nigger teacher down at Sandy Run. He looks like a white man, don't he, Mandy?"

"Niggers is niggers," said Mandy, "and looks don't make 'em white."

Mandy's own position was too uncertain to permit any latitude in regard to niggers. People who were born white and could prove it might afford to be liberal in their views on the matter of blood, but Mandy had the zeal of the proselyte.

"My mammy won't let me speak to niggers," said the girl.

"I should think not," said Mandy, emphatically.

It was the day following this, and just a week after their first meeting that Lowrey got speech with her again. He dismissed school early. His pupils went away, all except the inevitable Rose Amelia, who was last in her seat, and loitered at the door.

"Don't wait for me, Rose Amelia," said the teacher.

Rose Amelia went away disappointed, but the teacher's manner plainly intimated that he had dismissed her because he wanted to be alone. Her disappointment made her sad, until she saw a rabbit run across the road. She gave chase, but the rabbit disappeared in the woods, and Rose Amelia kept along the highway until she came to the road leading to the plankroad, when she remembered that she had once found some very fine chinquapins a little way down this path. She turned aside, and had begun gathering the prickly triangular nuts from the chinquapin bushes bordering the road, when she heard the heavy footsteps of some one approaching at a run. With Rose Amelia it was a natural instinct to conceal herself behind the bushes, and look out to see who was coming. It was but a moment until she saw her teacher pass by at a sharp run, going toward the Lumberton road.

Now, Rose Amelia was a preternaturally sharp little girl in some respects, and it required no appreciable moment of time for her to conclude—it was a perception, rather than a conclusion—that Lowrey was not running from mere excess of animal spirits, or for exercise. There was an expression of hope and determination in his face that would have made it clear to a less discerning person than Rose Amelia that he had a purpose in view, and was bent upon an errand he considered of importance.

Rose Amelia was by nature inquisitive. She had often gone to much trouble to find out other people's affairs from mere curiosity. But she loved her teacher, and felt a personal interest in his movements, and a keen pang of jealousy shot through her at the thought that he could have any interests in Sandy Run that she was not cognizant of. Her impulse was to follow him and find out his errand. She was not restrained by the refined sentiment of honor supposed to prevail among people who have had superior opportunities to hers. It did occur to her for a moment that her teacher might not like her to follow him. But she disposed of this consideration by a very simple philosophy: if he did not know it, he would be none the wiser, and she none the less in his favor—a method of reasoning not altogether unknown among people much superior to Rose Amelia in training and station.

She judged from his pace and from his straightforward gaze that he meant to go some distance. Rose Amelia was familiar with every road for miles around. By taking a short cut across a bend in the road she succeeded in heading Lowrey off about a quarter of a mile farther along, and then keeping in the underbrush, through which she passed rapidly and noiselessly, she kept him in sight until he reached the plankroad, where he came to a halt. When he stopped she drew back into a thicket and screened herself carefully from observation, keeping Lowrey well in view.

Chapter 7

*M*andy had parted from Lowrey at their former meeting very much disturbed in mind. For several months she had almost forgotten him. She had been angry at his desertion; but anger is a fleeting passion, and either dies entirely, or is succeeded by indifference, or hatred, or cold dislike. In her case it had become by degrees indifference. As long as she had remained in her old home, if he had returned she would have welcomed him gladly, and would have counted herself the happiest of women. But now she had given him up as lost to her, and had started out upon a new life, and her engagement with Lowrey was among the things that were cast behind. His sudden and entirely unlooked for reappearance had startled and alarmed her. She had a new lover, and this old one, if he sought to renew their former relations, would only embarrass her later love affair. Any intimacy or public association with Lowrey would entirely destroy her new social relations, and with them any hope of the marriage she dreamed of—for it was but little more than a dream—with her lover on horseback.

But since their meeting she had had time to compose her mind in some degree, and with returning equanimity came a flood of vivid recollections. She remembered how she had loved Lowrey, and how he had loved her; every kiss, every caress, every moonlight walk, the whole panorama of their year of love unrolled itself before her. She recalled their parting, and the evident pain it gave him; and it occurred to her that perhaps she had judged him harshly, that perhaps she had required too much in asking that he give up his hopes and his aspirations. And, after all, was it not for her sake that he had gone to seek fortune? And had she not been mistaken about his forgetfulness and his neglect, for was he not here, and had he not come to seek her? And mingled with these tender thoughts came too the very obvious consideration, which had escaped her in the agitation of their first meeting, that, whatever her future course, it would be well to speak Lowrey fair, since by a word, a breath, he could destroy the fragile fabric of her social standing.

The day after her meeting with Lowrey, and while these thoughts were coursing through her mind, she had met her rich lover. He dashed up on his black mare, and jumping down walked beside Mandy, leaving the intelligent animal to follow.

"Sweetheart," he said, seizing her hand and kissing it—for he had been well bred, and knew how to woo women—"you seem sad. Did you think I had forsaken you?"

"No," she answered with assumed coldness, "I wasn't thinking of you at all," which was true enough.

He seemed piqued at her unconcern.

"I'm always thinking of you," he said reproachfully.

"Oh, indeed!" she said. "No one would think it. I hain't seen you for two whole days."

He laughed, and pressed her hand, which he had retained in his own. "Now, I know you love me," he said. "You say two days as if it were two years. But it has been a long time," he sighed, "and a dreary time."

"A *very* dreary time, no doubt, for you," she said; "I've heard something about you since we met last."

"What is it?" he asked eagerly. Then lightly, "Something nice, I know."

"I reckon you think it nice to have two girls, but I don't. I've heard that you're engaged to be married to your cousin."

He looked seriously annoyed.

"And so you have heard that old story," he said. "But don't believe all you hear. The engagement is not of my making, and is not my wish, and I don't intend to keep it. The fact is, it is a property arrangement, and I have no intention of selling myself for money."

"But I hear the weddin' is to be next month."

"That ain't true; the wedding will never be."

Robert Utley was a true prophet, even with a lie on his lips.

"It is difficult to explain now, but there are reasons, good reasons, why I can't break this engagement for several weeks yet, until I get my affairs in such shape that I can snap my fingers at the rest of the world. It's a family scheme, and I don't intend to be the victim of it. I know," he said tenderly, as he put his arm around her, "I know a little woodland flower who is sweeter and fairer and dearer, and worth ten times more to me than that proud piece of millinery. Just wait, darling, until I am free of these cursed toils, and we shall—we shall—see. I will marry no woman but the woman I love."

She had at first repulsed him. But he was a man, and he was handsome and ardent, and he had been much in her thoughts, and she let his arm rest around her waist. Tall, dark, with clean-cut, aristocratic features, and a reckless, devil-may-care expression in his black eyes, he was a man from whom women at first shrank instinctively. But there was a fascination in the glitter of his eye, a charm in his flattering tongue, a seduction in his smile, that few women could in the end resist. He was not popular among men. They held him to be cold, and selfish and treacherous, and his friends were few. But to Mandy he represented that great, rich, powerful white world of which she dreamed, and to enter which since meeting him she had dared to aspire.

He wanted to lead her off into a by-road and prolong their interview. But she would not leave the main highway, and they walked along together until, at sight of a carriage approaching in the distance he kissed her, and, springing on his horse, set spurs to the spirited creature and soon disappeared down the road.

Mandy kept close to the roadside as the carriage approached, and when it was near her, stepped into the thicket, but not so quickly as to prevent her being seen. There were two women in the carriage, a white-haired lady, dressed quietly in gray, and a tall, proud-looking young woman, in a dress of some dainty summer stuff that set off her stately beauty. It was the aunt and cousin of her lover. And while Mandy envied the other woman her beauty—not knowing that she herself was more beautiful still—and her wealth, and her station; she yet consoled herself with the exulting reflection that Utley preferred her to this cold, proud cousin, and that when the wedding day arrived the cousin would not be the bride.

But it was yet several days before she next saw Lowrey, and her thoughts veered around again to him. Mandy was not fickle, but the situation was one to try any woman's heart. A woman's heart, like a weathercock, points steadily and true as long as the current of affection runs in one direction. But Mandy's feelings were in the variable state, now settling this way, and now that, as reason, recollection, ambition, passion, had each for the moment the upper hand. It seemed a pity that Lowrey's search should be in vain. When the fascination of her other lover's presence no longer exerted itself, she could compare the two men to better advantage. Lowrey did not dress so well, nor was he so polished. But he was a handsome man, and had a masterful way; and women like a master. And he was of her people; if she married him he would know all about her, and love her none the less. If she married the other, she would be in constant fear lest he should discover her antecedents, which might mean ruin. Lowrey was poor, but he had learning, he was even now further along in the world than when he had gone away to school. If she had not met the other, it would have been a rise in the world to marry Tom Lowrey. He was as white, in looks at least, as the other, and she might persuade him to do as she had done, and be entirely white, so far as the rest of the world was concerned.

Mandy was essentially human and essentially feminine. The upshot of her reflections was that she did not dislike Lowrey; that as men purely, she would scarcely know which to chose; that she would marry Utley, with his money and his position, if she could; but that she would hold Lowrey in reserve, and if Utley married his cousin, she would take Lowrey, after making him do reasonable penance for his former neglect. If she could have foreseen the result she might have hesitated before thus trying to carry water on both shoulders. But she had practically reached this conclusion when, on her way home from school, she saw Lowrey, a week after their first meeting, standing waiting for her at the end of the Sandy Run road. She did not see Rose Amelia, hidden in the chapparal.

Chapter 8

"*H*ow d'ye do, Mandy." Lowrey spoke with a humbly apologetic air, more or less sincere. He wanted to humor her mood, and it was safest to assume it most unfavorable to himself.

"Good evenin', " she said stiffly, and made as if to pass on by.

"Are you in a hurry?" he pleaded.

She turned, and with the side of her face toward him, replied:

"Well, that depen's on whether I've got any 'casion to stop. Mammy'll have supper ready when I get home. I'll have to hurry."

"I'll go with you," he said eagerly, throwing prudence to the winds.

"'Deed you won't," she said. "You forget I'm white, an' you're colored."

"I forget everything but you. If I can't go with you, come and walk down this quiet path with me. No one will see us."

She had refused to walk down that road with Robert Utley a few days before; but she had no fear of Lowrey. To walk on quiet roads with him was an old habit. Nevertheless she did not want to consent too readily.

"Why should I go to walk with you? The last time you spoke to me you insulted me, an' I'm mad with you."

"I take it all back, Mandy. I could have cut out my tongue the minute after I said it. Do come."

"What do you want to tell me?"

"I want to tell you how sorry I am that I went away and stayed so long, and seemed to neglect you."

They had turned into the road, and he was now talking eagerly, and passionately.

"I want to tell you how much I love you, dear, and to ask you to forgive me, and take me back."

She shook her head. "It's easy to talk, Tom Lowrey; but actions speak louder than words. You like me when you see me, and when I'm gone you forget me."

"I think of you all the time. When I give out the words in the spelling-book they all seem to spell 'Mandy.' When the children say the multiplication table, five times five, six times six, seven times eight, all give the same product—'Mandy.' When I ask what is the highest mountain or the largest sea, the answer comes to me before they can reply—'Mandy.' For you are all the world to me."

Mandy's forced severity could not resist such egregious flattery.

"Oh, Tom," she said, "you talk better than you used to. If you had talked like that to me down in Sampson I never would have let you go away. But it's too late now," she added, viciously, "You had your chance, and you didn't take it."

"Don't say that, darlin'," he pleaded, as he sought to take her hand. But she put her hands behind her, and kept him away.

"I know now," she said, "why you forgot me. You were goin' with some other girl. No man can talk like that without practice."

He flushed slightly, and, she thought, guiltily. There was a young woman that lived near the college—but it had never amounted to anything.

"Do you think I could look at another woman," he said, "after I had known you? Do you imagine I could find any one as sweet, and as pretty, as you?"

"I think a good many things," she said coldly. "I'm older than I was when you went away from Sampson County. I thought then that men were faithful and true, and that love meant somethin' great and grand and lastin'. You learned me different."

"No, Mandy, I swear I never loved anybody but you, and never shall. Say you love me, darlin'. Give me another chance," he pleaded.

She shook her head and moved away from him.

"Ef I did," she said, "you would kiss me—"

"Of course I would. I will now."

"No, you don't," she said as she pushed him away. "And then when your school was over, you would go back to college, and you would forget me. And you would la'f to think what a pore, simple fool I had been. No, Tom Lowrey, even a rabbit"—one ran across the road in front of them as she said it—"wouldn't be caught twice in the same trap."

"I swear I would never leave you. I would marry you, and never a day should we be apart; and I would work for you, I would live for you, and if need be I would die for you."

She could not doubt his earnestness, and her heart throbbed exultantly at his protestations. It was sweet to be courted in this fashion. But the image of the other man came before her, and she found herself comparing them, and wondering which was the better wooer. There was no doubt as to which was the more earnest of the two. She felt that she could love Lowrey again if she would, and that she would if she did not speedily bring this interview to an end. She had mapped out her course, and she must not go too fast. She turned and started back to the plankroad.

"I must go now," she said. "Mammy'll be waitin' for me."

"Say one kind word to me, Mandy."

"I'll think about it," she replied. "It'll take a right smart thinkin' to overlook them two years. Good-bye. Don't come out to the main road. Somebody might see us."

Somebody did see them. Rose Amelia, from her hiding place, had seen the whole interview, had watched the play of their faces. No movement had escaped her, and with precocious wisdom she had read Mandy's face better than Lowrey could, and had trembled at what she saw. And as for Lowrey's countenance, it was an open book. Rose Amelia had tried to get near enough to hear what was said, but could not without risk of discovery.

But she had seen enough. When Mandy turned to go homeward, Rose Amelia, to whom she was a stranger, hesitated as to whether to follow the teacher, or to follow this white girl, and find out who she was and where she lived. But Lowrey proved the stronger attraction, and as he walked slowly homeward, somewhat depressed in spirits, but not without hope of success, a little black figure crept silently behind him in the underbrush. And when their ways parted, Rose Amelia, torn with jealousy, full of rage against the fair enchantress who had bewitched her teacher, went to the miserable cabin she called her home, and far into the night, on her pallet on the floor, wept bitter tears, and turned over wild schemes of revenge.

Chapter 9

On the following Sunday Lowrey went to Sandy Run Church in the morning, and remained to Sunday School. He spent the afternoon at home. Several visitors came in, among them Mr. Absalom Revels. And with reading and writing and conversation the long, dull afternoon wore away.

"Is yer heard 'bout de big revival gwine on at de camp-meetin'?" asked Mr. Pate, at the supper table.

"Up at Snow Hill Church?" He had heard there was a camp-meeting up at the white church.

"Yes. Dey's done had mo'd'n a hund'ed under conviction, an' twenty-five or thirty has done come th'ough. Dey's be'n a mighty outpourin' er de Sperrit—I reckon dey need's it, ef dey *is* white folks. An' dey's invited de colored folks to come, an' dey gwine ter have a big time ter-night. Me an' some er de chil'en is gwine over. Would you lack ter go?"

"I don't think I care to go," said Lowrey. He very rarely went among white people. He had never served them in any menial capacity, and he was so nearly one of them that it always aroused in him a sort of dull resentment at being treated as an inferior creature. He reasoned with himself to overcome this feeling, as unworthy of him, and showing a want of self-respect. He knew he was as white as they, he believed he was the superior of many of them, in intellect, in culture, in energy; and he tried to look down, with a fine philosophic scorn, upon the unworthy prejudice that condemned him to hopeless social inferiority. But, after all, human nature was stronger than philosophy, and he never went where white people were without feeling as though he were being robbed of his birthright. He often wondered whether darker people experienced the same feeling in the same degree; or whether the fact that he was so near the line gave it special poignancy in his case. It was inconvenient too, sometimes, to be so white. White people who did not know him were apt to treat him as one of themselves, and if he acquiesced, and they subsequently learned the contrary, they were likely to blame him for presumption rather than themselves for lack of discernment. He was liable to hear people express freely, in the supposed presence of an equal, their opinions of colored people, which were often the reverse of complimentary. But in spite of these disagreeable features of his position, he had never felt the inclination to give up his people, and cast in his lot with the ruling caste. His feelings were not entirely within his control, but his actions were, and there was something repugnant to him in the idea of concealment. Not that he thought he would be wronging anyone else, for he had always felt instinctively, that he had a right to the same God-given opportunities as any other man. But he had nothing to be ashamed of. He was not responsible for his drop of dark blood. He had come by it honestly, for his father and mother, who were both of his own class, had been lawfully wedded. He had never been a slave, nor so far as tradition told of his ancestry, had he ever had a slave ancestor. And though his mixed blood implied both slavery and illegitimacy, the taint of both was remote enough not to bring any special sense of shame or humiliation on account of either. He believed in himself, he hoped to make a man of himself, he even dreamed of fame, this low-caste boy, in the back-woods of one of the most backward States of the Union; and he did not wish ever to be ashamed of or to blush for his origin. He reasoned that if he ever accomplished any great or worthy deed the world would learn his antecedents anyway; if he never amounted to anything, it was merely a choice of mud-puddles, whether he should be a white tadpole or a black one; and that if he climbed up in life to any considerable altitude, the fact that he had started low would not detract from the merit of his success.

Deacon Pate and "some er de chil'en"—some six or eight of them—set out after supper for the camp-meeting. Lowrey sat out in the yard for an hour in the twilight, until it occurred to him that Mandy might be at the camp-meeting. It was stupid in him not to have thought of it before, but he had never got quite accustomed to thinking of Mandy as a white woman. He sprang from his chair, and started for the camp-meeting.

His way lay along the same road up which he had gone so often with the hope of meeting Mandy. Night had fallen. The evening air was vocal with the shrill chirp of the cicada, and the croaking of small frogs, to which now and then some monarch of the pond added his deep bass; and far away the melancholy note of the screech-owl came faintly through the forest. The moon was shining, but the narrow road running as it did through the unbroken forest, was deep in shadow, except here and there where the moon cast fantastic spots of yellow light through the tree tops.

He turned at length into the plankroad. Walking rapidly, he passed several groups of people on their way to the meeting, weird shadowy shapes in the moonlight, and soon reached Snow Hill Church.

Snow Hill Church was a small frame structure, used as a school-house during the few months of the year that the public schools were open; as a meeting place for the rare occasions when public political gatherings were required in the township; and as a church on Sundays, when a preacher's services could be procured. For the past few weeks a wandering John-the-Baptist had held forth nightly, preaching with a force and earnestness that had attracted large audiences and resulted in many conversions. There had been no such religious awakening in the township for many years.

The church had proved too small for the crowds that attended nightly, and the services were therefore held in the open air, or rather under a rude canopy of pine boughs built in one day by the preacher and a few volunteers assisting him. The pulpit had been brought out and placed at one end of the improvised temple, as had been also the rude benches, made from slabs, or the rough outside pieces of pine logs sawed up in the neighboring sawmill. These benches were without backs, and stood on legs composed of sticks inserted in holes bored at suitable angles, the ends of the sticks sometimes projecting above in a way to require care in seating one's self. Pine logs had been placed longitudinally on the sides of the auditorium, to furnish additional seating capacity, and the clearing around afforded abundant standing room.

The seats were filled when Lowrey arrived, and he contented himself by leaning against a post in the rear and looking at the congregation. Three-fourths of them were white, the white people of the sand-hills. Most of the women were clad in homespun, with now and then a girl resplendent in figured calico. The men were mostly bearded, round-shouldered, and had not deemed it necessary to intermit the chewing of tobacco during the religious service. On one side a place was set aside for colored worshippers. This was out of the common, the colored people having their own churches and preferring to attend them. But the fame of the evangelist had spread so far that it was decided that if the negroes desired, they should be permitted to hear him. A place was also provided where negro mourners could come forward to be prayed for. The portion set aside for colored people was well filled, and a goodly number were standing on the outside. While there was some conversation going on in subdued tones, there were no whites and blacks conversing together.

Running his eye over the congregation Lowrey soon saw Mandy, though, as he was behind her, she did not observe him. She was sitting about half way from the front, on the white side of the house, at the point farthest removed from the colored people.

Someone touched Lowrey on the shoulder. He turned, and recognized Julius Peak, the father of one of his pupils.

"Come out to de meetin', is ye?" said Mr. Peak.

"Yes, I thought I'd hear Elder Gadson."

"He's a powerful speaker. He's made more converts 'n ary preacher 't ever spoke here."

Peak was going on to give further details of Elder Gadson's achievements, when the preacher himself, accompanied by two deacons, came from the darkness into the dim circle of light cast by the tallow candles stuck around on the posts holding up the roof. He was a tall, loose-jointed man, lean almost to emaciation, with a full beard, and with deep-set, glistening eyes, the eyes of devotees and fanatics and the insane. He wore a suit of rusty black, coarse shoes, a homespun shirt with a turn-down collar, and a black cravat carelessly knotted; and when he knelt before the rude pulpit for a moment of silent prayer, Lowrey saw that his sandy hair was thin, and that his forehead was very high and very narrow. The face was that of a man of strong passions, but of weak will; when will and passion worked together, a great power for good or for evil, as the case might be. Hitherto they had combined to work for the welfare of others.

The minister rose, and the audience rustled with a moment of preparation and then subsided into silence. The minister opened a hymn-book, at which he did not look again, and gave out a hymn, two lines at a time:

Alas! and did my Savior bleed
And did my Sovereign die.

He then began to sing in an old-fashioned, wailing tune. The congregation took it up, and the weird volume of sound floated out into the night and echoed far into the forest. Lowrey felt himself filled with an almost indescribable melancholy.

The hymn ceased, and silence deep and profound fell upon the congregation, broken only by the impatient neighing of a horse tied to a neighboring tree.

"Let us draw near the throne of grace."

With a simultaneous movement the congregation dropped to their knees, and the preacher prayed:

"Oh, Lord, our heavn'ly Father, we draw neah to thy th'one of grace this ev'nin. Fer we know that we are all mis'able sinners, an' are not wo'thy to be called thy child'n. We know that we have disobeyed thy comman'ments, an' that we have no claims of our own upon thy mussy. We know that the mouth o' hell is yawnin' fer us, that the flames o' torment are even now risin' up roun' us, that thy wrath is hangin' over us, an' will fall an' smite us ef we do not turn from our wicked ways an' cast our sins on thee."

The preacher went on in this strain, working himself into a frenzy of penitence and humiliation. As he neared the end of the prayer his voice broke, and the last few despairing words were sobbed out. The audience groaned and quivered in sympathy, and the long-drawn out "Amen!" was joined by a hundred voices.

A few notices were then given out by a deacon, and after that another hymn, more mournfully despairing, was sung to a sadder and more depressing tune than the first, and with a deeper intensity of feeling. Lowrey was filled with strange emotions, and a sense of his own sinfulness oppressed him. Then the preacher spoke. His text was the familiar one:

"Flee from the wrath to come."

He might have been some ancient Hebrew prophet or some mediaeval monk as he stood before them, his long figure towering above the pulpit, his eyes shining with an inner light, his skinny hands now clasped in supplication, now pointed in emphasis, now shaken in denunciation. He began by telling them what God had done for them, and then showed them how they had requited his goodness by ingratitude and sin. He spoke in the accent of the sand-hills; not the smooth, oily dialect

of the negro, but differing from it only in the sense of being somewhat more grammatical and spoken with less unctuousness.

Then the preacher, warming to his subject, invoked the wrath of God upon the impenitent. He pictured the fate of the damned; John Wesley himself could not have described with greater detail their pangs and tortures. Lowrey felt himself shiver and turn pale at the Dantesque particularity and gloom of the preacher's descriptions. It was uncanny, and he struggled to shake off the impression that pervaded him. He thought he would walk away into the woods for a moment until he recovered his mental equilibrium; but the sermon fascinated him. The preacher's eye seemed to pierce the gloom and fix itself upon him alone, and he could not move, as the anathemas of the preacher thundered around him. For a time he even forgot Mandy's presence, and saw only the nightmare that had been conjured up.

The audience sat in shuddering horror, which even the incongruous cry of an old colored woman, "Glory to de Lam'!" could not disturb; and soon groans and sobs and smothered shrieks began to be audible here and there.

Then the preacher's voice softened, and with tears in his eyes, and in tones broken by emotion, he told how Christ had died for them, how he had given up the glories of Heaven and taken upon himself the burden of life:

"Yes, my hearers, the burden o' life. For what is life but one long battle? We air bawn, we struggle for a little bread an' a little meat, an' a few rags to cover us. We flutter in the worl' a few years like a candle in the win', an' we go out."

He painted in tones of marvellous tenderness the love of Jesus, and the joys of paradise; and then when the audience were sobbing like so many children, he towered to his full height and again invoked in harsh tones the wrath of God, and warned sinners to flee from it.

"Flee from the wrath ter come, my hearers. An' while we sing, let ev'ry sinner come to the th'one o' grace. Come ter the anxious seat, the white people on the seats to the right an' after them the black people to the lef'. For God is no respecter o' pussons. Whatever may be best on airth, in the jedgmen' day thar'll be no rich, no po', no white, no black, but all sinners, trembling in the presence of their righteous God. Come one, come all. Sinner man, sinner woman, now is the opportunity, now is the hour, now is the accepted time, now is the day of salvation!"

With a burst of perfervid eloquence the preacher sat down. One of the deacons started a hymn, and the congregation sang, the colored

portion of the audience contributing the greater volume of sound, in spite of their smaller numbers.

The front benches were cleared, and the mourners quickly filled them. It required an effort for Lowrey to restrain his own inclination to join them. He would not have believed, after his years of study, that he could be so affected, and his attitude of mind was the highest compliment to the preacher's eloquence. Lowrey stood and looked over the heads of those in front of him and watched the mourners go up. Some went slowly, as if against their will; others eagerly, as if to unburden themselves. Some were tearful, as if their hearts had been touched, and they must find repose. Others were cold, as if they had merely been logically convinced of impending damnation, and felt it wise to try to avoid it. A murmur of whispered prayers flowed out upon the night air, swelling into a louder hum as the penitents grew more earnest and more abandoned in their grief and self-abasement.

When the hymn was over there was a prayer, led by one of the brethren who felt that he possessed a gift in that direction. He prayed for the righteous and he prayed for sinners. He prayed for the absent and the present, the sick and the afflicted, the oppressed and the distressed; for the brethren and the sisters, the young and the old, the white and the black, the rich and the poor, the wise and the foolish; for the souls of the heathen who died in ignorance of the true faith; for unborn generations. He prayed for the congregation collectively and severally, and prayed at some length for himself as one in especial need of divine help. He prayed so long that the congregation tired, and the preacher, by a dexterous flank movement, cut him off with a sonorous "Amen" at which the audience rose with a rustle of relief. Then the elder added a brief exhortation to those who had not yet come forward, and started another hymn.

In the momentary lull between two verses of the hymn, Lowrey heard a footstep approaching in the gloom, and a moment later a man came up to the edge of the canopy and looked in. The newcomer then stepped forward and took a place a few feet in front of Lowrey.

When Lowrey looked toward the pulpit, his line of vision lay over this man's shoulder, and as he turned his eyes in that direction he saw Mandy Oxendine get up from the white side of the house. He became aware at the same moment that the stranger too had recognized her, for the latter uttered a smothered exclamation that sounded very much like an oath. Mandy went forward and knelt among the white mourners, at the end of the bench farthest from the colored side.

Chapter 10

*W*hen Mandy, in going forward to the mourners' bench, had come into the brighter circle of light immediately surrounding the pulpit, the preacher's eye fell upon her, and lingered for a moment. Not even the strong emotions, the tense excitement of the hour, could prevent his glance from resting on a face, which by virtue of its beauty, stood out in striking contrast to those around it. Most of the women present were of the prevalent sand-hill type—listless, for want of eventfulness in their lives; pale and anaemic for want of nourishing and varied food; and not infrequently yellowed from excessive use of tobacco; with lank figures and sandy hair, lack-lustre eyes and expressionless faces. Even the younger women but foreshadowed the maturer type. In the crowd and in the obscurity of the dimly lighted tabernacle, the preacher had not especially noticed Mandy. But as her tall figure drew near the pulpit and he caught sight of her face, marked by the emotions his own eloquence had evoked, she appeared before him as a revelation of something hitherto unseen and unknown. A man of powerful imagination, he had never before this been especially moved by one of the opposite sex. While he had taken no vow of asceticism, until the fatal moment when his eye fell upon Mandy Oxendine, he had lived the life of a zealot; he had denied himself pleasure and comfort, had fasted and prayed, and had let his fancy dwell upon celestial delights and infernal

pains, to the exclusion of earthly joys and sorrows. For some months he had been conducting revival meetings, and the strain of constant labor and excitement had not been without its effect upon a mind, whose powers, though naturally fine, had never been subjected to the discipline of scholastic training. So it was that when Mandy's image appeared to him, it was to a heart untouched by love, and to a mind in a state of unnatural and almost dangerous exaltation. Unsought, unthought of, unknown, this slender girl stepped forward into the light from the pulpit, and simultaneously into the heart of the preacher.

He did not know at first what had happened to him. He thought the thrill that shot through him was but an access of religious emotion, or a special outpouring of the Divine presence. A few moments later he stooped down to whisper words of encouragement into the ear of the penitent.

"Pray, my sister. Whatsoever ye ast, believin', the Lawd will give it to ye'. Pray hahd, my sister."

He did not know that the odor of her hair exhilarated him. He thought of her then as a beautiful sinner, a brand to be plucked from the burning, another jewel for his Lord's crown.

Meantime Mandy prayed, and prayed in vain. Under the burning words of the preacher she had felt an oppressing sense of sinfulness, and she sought at the altar to find, not at first forgiveness, but repentance. But the tears would not come, her prayers seemed mere mechanical repetitions. The voice of the preacher, the sobs of the mourners, the wailing cadences of penitential hymns, all fell upon an irresponsive ear. And when the preacher, passing along the line of mourners, in a moment of great fervor, laid his hand on her head as he exhorted her to greater self-abandonment, she shrunk from his touch, and found herself a moment later looking at him through her fingers with a hardly recognized feeling of dislike and repulsion. She could not tell why she shrunk from him, nor why as she felt his eyes fixed on her, she felt an almost irresistible impulse to get up and go away. But she kept her place until the last hymn had been sung, the last prayer prayed and the benediction pronounced. And when the meeting broke up she started homeward, unconscious of the fact that two men were watching her, and that she had remained behind in the heart of a third.

Mandy started away alone. Part of the congregation had gone ahead of her, and she could see their forms outlined in the moonlight, and hear the faint sounds of their voices, one still praying, one exhorting, and others whose voices were but an indistinct murmur. There were others behind whom she knew would have to come her road and who would doubtless soon follow, so that the way would not be lonely. She did not wait for them. She knew them only casually, and was not in a mood for conversation or companionship. She was not timorous, and crimes of violence were so rare on the sandhills that no thought of danger occurred to her.

Lowrey had not at first joined her as she left the tabernacle. Just before the meeting closed he had drawn back a little from the light, so as to avoid Peak or Pate, one or both of whom he thought might be expecting him to go with them. Besides wishing to avoid their company, he knew that Mandy would not care to be seen with them.

The other man doubtless had his own reasons for remaining in the background. But whatever the reasons were, they lost their weight as soon as Mandy was alone and beyond the circle of light that the few expiring candles still made around the meeting-place. Mandy was not yet out of the clearing, and her slender figure was clearly outlined in the moonlight, when casting a hasty glance around to see that he was not observed, he sprang rapidly forward, overtook her, and was immediately swallowed up with her in the deep shadows on one side of the road.

When the late-comer had moved forward to join Mandy, Lowrey had already quickened his pace with the same object; but seeing himself forestalled he uttered an impatient exclamation under his breath and set out after the retreating pair. He soon came close behind them. The sandy road gave no sound of his footsteps, and by closely hugging the woods at the roadside he could keep them in view and still be himself effectually screened from sight. He had on dark clothing, which merged into the dark background, while Mandy and her escort were clad in light garments that marked them distinctly.

Lowrey did not try to get near enough to overhear their conversation. Not that he would not have liked to hear it, but it savoured too much of spying. If he had been a husband, he thought, or an accepted lover, he would have had no scruples; but being merely one of two aspirants, a love of fair play as well as a sense of self-respect kept him from listening to what they said. He could accomplish his purpose just as well by merely keeping them in sight. He had no confidence in the good faith or honesty of purpose of Mandy's other lover, and he meant to see her safely home. If she should need a friend before her mother's door closed upon her, he would be at hand. He had with him a stout stick which he always carried when he went out at night, and which would make a very effective weapon in a contest between man and man.

The couple in front of him walked slowly, and ere long turned from the main highway into the path leading to Mandy's home. The road was narrow, the shadows deep, but Lowrey could have sworn that an arm encircled Mandy's waist. A hot wave of jealousy swept over him, and he unconsciously clutched harder the stick he held in his hand. They walked slowly, and it was with growing impatience that Lowrey slackened his pace so as to maintain his distance from them.

By and by they stopped in the shadow of the trees just across the road from the bars in front of Mandy's house. The murmur of the man's voice fell upon Lowrey's ear. He was speaking rapidly and earnestly, and in pleading tones. All Lowrey's jealous instincts awoke, and grasping his stick more tightly he drew nearer to the unsuspecting pair. He saw Mandy shake her head and heard her say "No" with emphasis. The lover grew more insistent, and tightened his arm about her waist. Lowrey, growing more and more impatient, was just on the point of interfering, when Mandy, with a sudden movement, broke away from the encircling arm and with a spring like that of a deer bounded across the road, leaped lightly over the bars and ran up the path to the door.

"Good-night," came fluttering down the path in a ripple of laughter. There was no trace in her voice of the mood of the hour before.

"Good-night, sweetheart, and dreams of me," responded the man in a tone that did not entirely conceal his discomfiture.

"D____n you, my pretty, I'll have you yet," he muttered, as, all unconsciously, he passed close by where Lowrey stood behind the trunk of a great pine tree. "But I must make haste, or this infernal wedding will take me away for a month, and in love a month is a lifetime."

"And d____n you, my scoundrel," said Lowrey to himself, "you shall not have her if I can prevent it. If you had held her a moment longer, or she had manifested the least alarm, it would have been several days before you could have used your arm again."

He thought, as Utley walked away, how easy it would be to creep up behind him and strike him a blow that would render him unconscious or disarm him by the surprise, and then vent his jealousy on him by a good beating. The night would conceal his face, and Utley would have no reason to suspect the identity of his assailant. But he put the thought aside as unworthy; it might have occurred to any one, but not every one would have dismissed it so promptly. He let Utley go on ahead of him, following him at a short distance until they gained the plankroad, along which his own path and Utley's led in the same direction for about a quarter of a mile. When he reached the entrance to his own road he stopped a moment, and hearing Utley whistling ahead of him on the plankroad, knew that the coast was clear, and quickening his pace soon arrived at home.

Mr. Pate let him into the house.

"Laws-a-massy! Brer Lowrey, did yer git los' in de woods? Me an' de chil'en looked all roun' fer yer, an' couldn' see nothin' er yer, so we 'lowed yer'd done gone, an' so we come 'long home. I reckened likely yer had come down de road wid Brer Peak."

"We missed one another somehow," said Lowrey evasively. "Have you been home long?"

"'Bout half an hour," said Pate. "De chil'en is already gone ter sleep."

"Well, I'll go to sleep myself," said Lowrey.

He bade his host good-night, and without striking a light or making any unnecessary noise, which would have been audible all over the flimsily constructed house, he went to bed, but not immediately to sleep. He spent several hours in thinking how he could best watch over Mandy, protecting her from the other man and at the same time strengthening his own position.

Chapter 11

The preacher slept but little that night. Indeed he rarely slept after the excitement of an evening service. But the midnight hours were filled with visions of the beautiful young penitent who had knelt at his feet and upon whose braided hair he had laid his fevered palm. During all the next day he could scarcely think of anything else. He made inquiries about her in the neighborhood, and learned that she was a comparative stranger, living alone with her old mother. She attended the Snow Hill School, and was a bright and studious pupil. The more the preacher thought of her the harder it was to shake off those thoughts. He looked forward with eagerness to the church service on Sunday, and felt anxious and depressed until he saw her in the congregation. Her presence seemed to inspire him, and on Sunday morning he preached a sermon which became memorable in the annals of Snow Hill.

All the afternoon, though she was absent, the memory of her face pursued him. When the evening came and he had entered the pulpit, and said the brief prayer which custom demanded, he sent a searching glance over the congregation and felt a strange sinking at heart when he saw she was not there. He gave out the first hymn, and she had not appeared by the time it was sung. Sick with suspense, he did not feel equal to the prayer, and called upon one of the deacons to pray. And while the words of the deacon ascended to heaven, the thoughts of the minister wandered to Mandy. He wondered why she had not come; and in a vague and indefinite way it seemed to him as though the force of his own wish ought to have been strong enough to bring her, even against her own will. And when he finally gave up the hope of her coming a sense of irritation and surprise was mingled with his disappointment.

When the prayer was finished another hymn was sung, and then the preacher rose to preach. The words came with an effort. The tongue that had been wont to speak so eloquently, caught itself now and then hesitating for a figure, groping for a word, and it was with an effort that he could finish his discourse. The hours that on other days had been spent in prayer, had hitherto borne fruit in the intensely spiritual power of his sermons. To-day he had not prayed as usual, and Mandy's presence, to which he had looked for inspiration, had failed him. For he had meant to preach to her. He felt that he could almost have braved the hosts of hell single-handed to keep her from their clutches; or have borne off the gates of Heaven so that they might not be closed against her. The souls of these poor sandhillers seemed to him but dross, compared with the soul of the beautiful penitent upon whose brown hair he had laid his hand. The sermon was not a successful one. It did not entirely fail of effect, for the fame of the preacher was so great that many came prepared to admire, and saw no ground for criticism, and those who missed the fire and the flow of the morning's exhortation, felt that perhaps the difference was due to a reaction in themselves from the high tension of the morning. The service went on, and the mourners went up to be prayed for, and several were converted; and there was praying, and singing, and weeping and groaning and shouting. But while the preacher's voice was exhorting sinners to pray, his heart was elsewhere; and before he went to sleep that night, he decided that he would go and see Mandy, and urge her to attend the meetings and continue her prayers. For up to this time the preacher had only thought, or imagined he had only thought of her as a lost soul, which it was his duty to save from everlasting death.

As for Mandy, she had not thought of the preacher. She had not gone to meeting for several reasons. One was that her feelings had undergone a revulsion since Friday night, and as she was not in the mood to go forward to be prayed for, she did not care to attract the attention which remaining away from the mourner's bench would have drawn had she been present at the meeting. The preacher's eloquence that had fascinated her and drawn her irresistibly to the mourner's bench, had lost its effect in the clear light of day, and she even felt a little ashamed that she should have yielded so readily to her emotions. Such weakness was scarcely compatible with the difficult role she had assumed in respect to her two lovers, and she wished to avoid repetition of it. Another reason why she had not gone to meeting was that she was just the least bit afraid of her fine lover; at least she thought it best, after her experience of Friday night, to meet him hereafter in the daytime.

Chapter 12

Mandy might have spared her fears so far as Utley was concerned, for he was not at the campmeeting on Sunday night. In the afternoon he had gone over to Colonel Brewington's. His aunt, who was also Florence's aunt, was sitting on the porch reading a church paper. She would have regarded any other kind of paper as sinful for Sunday reading.

"Come in, Bob," she said, "and sit down. Ain't it hot?"

"Awfully hot. Where's Florence?"

"Florence is lying down. I'll call her directly, but not now. I have a crow to pick with you first."

"I don't know whether I've got a bag big enough to hold the feathers or not. You alarm me so that I'll have to smoke a cigar to quiet my nerves, if you don't mind."

"If you never did anything more objectionable than smoking, Bob, I would never need to trouble about you," she said half fondly and half reproachfully, for she loved her handsome scapegrace of a nephew.

Utley lit a cigar and stretched himself comfortably in a rocking-chair. "Now, what is it, auntie? I am prepared for the worst."

"You know perfectly well what it is, Bob. Have you forgotten the fact that you are to be married this Summer?"

"No, Aunt Hannah, I am fully aware of my impending doom. I

count the flying hours that intervene between youth and liberty and matrimonial chains."

"I believe you are half in earnest when you say that. Do you know that you are going to marry the handsomest woman in Marlborough County?"

"I believe that is the generally received opinion among the best people. I accept their judgment, and count myself lucky, since I must marry, to secure such a prize."

"And the richest girl in the country?"

"Undoubtedly correct. It is one of the most substantial and enduring of her charms."

"You don't know how she loves you, Bob."

"I am honored and flattered by her preference. I am not worthy of it."

"You never said a truer word. But I have hopes of you, Bob. You are my own brother's child, and I don't believe you would make a bad husband to such a wife, a wife to whom you would owe so much. For you don't forget that your interests, your credit and even your good name are dependent upon this marriage?"

"No, my debts are ever before me, and I presume it is only my prospects that keep my creditors off."

"All that being the case, Bob, don't you think you ought to pay a little more attention to your betrothed?"

"Really, Aunt Hannah, I had not meant to fail in my duty in that regard. I had an idea that Florence saw about as much of me as she cared for. She seems too proud and cold to indulge in ordinary human weaknesses."

"You take too much for granted. No woman likes to be neglected. Florence loves you, but she is proud, and would never say a word or give a sign. She may seem cold, but under her seeming coldness a wealth of love and devotion are hidden, which need but a little warmth to thaw them out. And by the way, I know there is one thing which she will not tolerate, and that is what I particularly wanted to speak to you about."

"And which of my many sins is that, dear aunt?" he inquired with lazy curiosity, as he watched a carefully directed smoke-ring rise to the ceiling of the piazza.

Mrs. Ochiltree did not reply for a moment, and then she asked a question.

"Who was the girl you were talking to last Friday, over on the Lumberton Road?"

"Who? I? Talking to a girl? Really, I don't remember all the girls I speak to. I never was afraid of a girl."

"Nobody ever accused you of any such weakness. But I think I can refresh your recollection. Florence and I were out driving last Friday, on the Lumberton Road, between the Mineral Spring and Snow Hill, and as we turned a bend in the road I caught a glimpse of a black horse just disappearing around another bend ahead of us, and if I am not very much mistaken, you were its rider. Fortunately, Florence just at that moment, was looking back at something which had attracted her attention, and did not see you. Knowing you as I do, and having your interests ever in mind, I said nothing to her of what I had seen. A moment later we passed a girl, a beautiful girl; not a lady, but a girl with a fine figure and a fine face. Who is she?"

"Why, my goodness, Aunt Hannah, how should I know? Are you sure it was I you saw?"

"Reasonably sure. I noticed as we drove along, the spot where Satan had stood pawing the ground while you conversed with this woodland nymph, and noticed his hoof-prints, which showed that you had galloped away, I presume when you heard us coming. I am too old a bird to be caught with chaff, Bob Utley. Who was the girl?"

"Well, now, that you have gone into detail and refreshed my recollection," said Utley, "I think I did pull Satan up a moment to ask a question of a young woman I met on the road. I had been over to—the sawmill, to see about some lumber, and I asked a girl if she had seen Colonel Kyle drive along the road."

"She was a very pretty girl," said Mrs. Ochiltree.

"Did Florence seem to think so?"

"Florence doesn't admire diamonds in the rough. When I observed that the girl was pretty, she replied that beauty was a matter of taste."

"A sage and trite remark, such as might be expected from the pupil of a fashionable boarding-school. Did the same unworthy suspicions enter her innocent mind that were engendered in your more sophisticated intellect?"

"Now, Bob Utley, don't be smart. I am experienced enough to read you like a book. I don't think Florence saw you or especially noticed the girl. I am your best friend, and you know it. I can't help you any more in your money matters, and you can take my word for it, that if you don't pay more attention to Florence she will throw you over. I can do so much with her but no more. She is anything but the commonplace schoolgirl that you seem to take her for. She is one of these quiet people, who do not carry their hearts upon their sleeves—"

" 'For daws to peck at,' " murmured Utley.

"But who can love or hate with equal intensity. She loves you, but she values her own self-respect still more; and if you slight or deceive her, she will neither forgive nor forget it."

"Aunt Hannah, say no more. I never saw this girl before, and shall probably never see her again, unless by accident. Call out the adorable Florence; I will do my duty like a man, and I think I know how."

Mrs. Ochiltree went into the house, and Florence soon appeared. She looked delightfully fresh and cool in a gown of some light, flowing material, confined at the waist by a white linen belt. Her abundant black hair was loosely and tastefully arranged. She had beauty of a stately, impressive type; she had refinement, style—everything, it would seem, that a reasonable man could wish. As Utley looked at her he thought what a graceful wife, what a perfect mother, what an excellent housekeeper she would make; not so cold as to be indifferent, not so affectionate as to be troublesome. But the very obviousness of her perfections impressed him with an uncomfortable sense of his own shortcomings. He could admire her, as he would a marble statue; but as for love, give him light heart, and bounding pulse and blooming cheek. He thought of Mandy, and seemed to hear her mocking laugh as she had last bid him good-night. And with a stifled sigh of regret he relinquished his project of visiting the camp-meeting, and devoted himself to serious love-making. To such an extent did he exert himself, and with such success, that the marble statue was warmed to life, Florence's dark cheek glowed, and her eyes grew limpid with the light of love.

Utley remained to supper and spent the evening at his cousin's. She deposed her aunt from the foot of the table and did the honors of the house herself. And after supper she played the piano, and sang to her lover and revealed to him in every tone and every glance that her heart was his whenever he chose to claim it. And when Utley strolled across to his own place at ten o'clock, he felt that from a practical point of view, his evening had been well spent, for his marriage was assured and his wedding day fixed.

But absence had only whetted his secret passion, and with Florence's kiss yet fresh upon his lips, and the perfume of her hair upon his cheek, he went to bed resolved to see Mandy again at the earliest opportunity, and press a suit which he feared or rather felt that his marriage would abruptly terminate.

When her lover had gone Florence Brewington sat long on the piazza, looking toward the house where he lived, and reproaching herself for having deemed him cold. She had thought him careless, overconfident, inattentive, and she had chafed under his neglect. Even her aunt's assurance that pressing business cares preoccupied him, had at length failed to satisfy her, and her patience was nearly at an end. But tonight he had been all that any woman could ask. His honeyed words had fallen like music on her ears. His delicate flatteries seemed but happy statements of things she had always known, and seemed to ratify her own good taste and discernment. He had called her beautiful and wise and proud. She still felt his kiss upon her lips, his arm around her waist. She saw herself a bride, arrayed in white, crowned with orange blossoms, standing at the altar, clasping her lover's hands and exchanging vows of eternal fidelity; and before her she saw stretching a long life of happiness, secure in the undisputed possession of her husband's love. For in her own undemonstrative way she had always loved her cousin and had wished no better fate than to become his wife.

And what a gallant, frank and manly fellow he was! He had been a little wild—while she was away at school, and before he had fallen under her compelling charm. But he had confessed to her his faults, and had promised that under her sweet and pure influence he would give up bad habits and evil associations and find pleasure in her and her only. He might have seemed cold, but it was only because he was not sure of her, and felt himself unworthy. He had not dreamt for a moment of presuming on that old family arrangement that had assigned them to one another. She knew that no mercenary consideration could ever have found place in so essentially noble a heart as his. And while she was not naturally trustful, such was Utley's art that he had not only given her confidence in himself, but had raised her own opinion of herself and her powers—a short and sure road to the human heart.

Chapter 13

Mandy was singing an old song, sung many years before by gallant cavaliers, and loyal ladies, when the debonair Stuart was wandering over England and France, hiding in country houses and making casual love to all the available damsels. And the Scotch exiles who with Flora Macdonald had settled on the Cape Fear, had brought it with them, and their children and grand-children had sung it, but none of them with a clearer note than this that floated out among the pines upon the morning air.

> Come bear me over, come carry me over,
>> Come carry me over to Charlie,
> I'll gie John Ross a bawbee more,
>> To carry me over to Charlie.

Mandy, hoe in hand, was working in the garden. It was the morning of the second day since her visit to the camp meeting. Her sun-bonnet had fallen back, disclosing her face, rounded with the tender and yet firm curves of lip and cheek and chin that mark the early twenties, and rosy with perfect health. Her abundant brown hair, brushed back from her temples, fell in a broad plait behind, almost to her feet. Her spirit had caught something of the freshness and beauty of the morning. The emotions stirred up, a few nights before, by darkness, flickering lights, morbid eloquence, and an exciting atmosphere, and the different feelings roused by her lover's caresses and burning words, had passed away, and she was experiencing the purely sensuous delight of mere living. And when after breakfast she had gone out to weed the garden, her joyfulness had found vent in song.

She sang on. A mocking-bird caroling to his mate from a neighboring tree, stopped short, and with head cocked to one side, listened attentively until Mandy reached the end of a stanza, when he caught up the closing strain, and repeating it once or twice by way of practice, embellished the theme with a hundred runs and thrills and melodious variations.

A man coming down the road, heard the song too, from afar. He quickened his pace at the sound, until he came in sight of the singer, when he stopped and listened with rapt attention.

"She sings like an angel," he said to himself, "she looks like an angel. But alas! she is a po' sinner, a los' soul, a bran' to be pluck' from the burnin'."

She stood erect, shook the sunbonnet entirely from her head, and looked fearlessly toward the sun, as she drank a deep draught of the morning air. The preacher, approaching on her left, as yet unperceived, caught her profile, and trembled as he watched the rise and fall of her bosom and the golden lights in her hair.

"Them bright eyes," he muttered, "which a few nights ago wuz filled with tears, is dry an' tearless now, and the prayer which fell from her rosy lips has give' place to sinful songs. Oh, my sister, how my soul yearns for yo' salvation."

Mandy had ceased her song, and as she worked, a shadow fell upon her pathway. She looked up and saw the preacher standing before her, his long lean arm extended.

"Good mornin', Sister Oxendine," he said, solemnly.

Again she felt the instinctive repulsion she had been conscious of when he had laid his hand upon her head at the mourner's bench, and it was with an effort that she lifted her arm and placed her fingers in his extended palm.

"Good mornin', Elder."

"I hope, my sister, that all is well with you this mornin'? Has the Lord spoke' to yo' soul, that you are so cheerful? Has the burden of sin rolled away from yo' heart? Is yo' joy breakin' forth in hymns of praise to God?"

Mandy was painfully embarrassed. She could not say a word, but colored furiously and lowered her eyes.

"Or," continued the preacher, reproachfully, "have you closed yo' ears to the voice of the Sperrit, an' has sin and worl'iness resumed their ol' sway, and have you put away repentance and prayer?"

Still no response from Mandy. She would have liked the earth to yawn and swallow her up. She felt a wild desire to run, but her feet were like lead; she could not lift them. She stood like a statue of guilt, and the sense of sin and self-reproach that his words awoke, was mingled with a vague fear of this man who could thus sway her mood.

"But, oh, remember, my sister," he went on, "that youth and lightness of heart, will pass away, and beauty will sho'ly fade. Yo' hair will whiten, an' yo' eyes will dim. An' in the dark days, when trouble an' sorrer come, you will wish you had come back to the camp-meetin' and searched for somethin' that time will not destroy. Will you come, my sister? Will you kneel again at the altar an' seek the best of all gif's?"

His voice stirred Mandy; she shrank from the man, but the power of the preacher was undeniable. She felt his eyes fixed upon her, and some subtle emanation of his will compelled her to look up.

"I'll come again to-night," she said. "Pray fer me, that I may find forgiveness for my sins."

"I'll wrastle on my knees in prayer an' besiege the th'one of grace all day long for you," he replied with fervor. "Yo' po' sinful soul is mo' precious in the sight of God than yo' beautiful young face in the sight o' man. I would give anything but my own hope of heaven to see yo' soul saved from everlastin' damnation."

He shook hands with her again, and once more it was with an effort that she bore the touch of his burning palm.

"Good-bye, my sister. To-night."

"Good-bye, Elder Gadson. I'll come."

She watched him as he walked slowly away, turning once or twice for a backward glance. She felt relieved when he was gone, but could not entirely shake off the gloom his presence had left upon her spirit. She sang no more, but continued her work in silence, until her mother called her into the house.

"Who was that man, Mandy?" she asked.

"It was Elder Gadson, that's runnin' the camp-meetin' at Snow Hill."

"What did he want, honey?"

"Wanted me ter come ter the revival and keep on tryin' ter get religion."

"My ear was burnin' all the mornin'," said her mother, "and I knowed somebody was comin'. But a hawk circled aroun' the house three times an' I expected bad luck. Is he a good man, chile?"

"He is a powerful preacher, mammy, an' has made many converts."

"Well, maybe the hawk wuz after chickens, but I never knowed the sign ter fail. Git religion, honey; it's a good thing ter have, an' a young gal is likely ter need it."

Mandy meantime had busied herself about the house. In dusting the mantlepiece in their sitting-room she accidentally knocked down a small hand-mirror that had been standing somewhat insecurely. It fell to the hearth, and while not shattered, was cracked across its full width.

"The hawk was right, Mandy. One sign might fail, but two never do. There's bad luck goin' ter happen ter this house. Ef yer go out-o'-doors an' walk roun' the house backwards three times yer may keep some of it off. But you'd better git religion, chile, fer you'll need it when trouble comes."

"Mammy, you're too superstitious. Our teacher says them ole-timey signs an' omens an' conjurations don't mean anything, that it's foolish an' sinful ter believe in 'em."

"Yo' teacher may know all 'bout readin' an' writin', an' cipherin', but he don't know nothin' 'bout signs. Yo' pappy brung a hoe in the house, an' he died inside of a month. Yo' brother Jim, when he was a baby, raised a' umbrella in the house, an' he fell into a barrel of water an' was drownded nex' day. I broke a lookin'-glass in the Spring, an' in the Summer the war broke out, an' the country was ruined. I've be'n sorry ever sence, an' ef I could 'a' had any idee w'at wuz goin' ter happen, I'd a be'en mo' keerful. Git ready fer trouble, chile, and w'en it comes, remember that yo' ole mammy knows some things that yo' school-teacher don't."

Chapter 14

The week following the night when he had witnessed Mandy's parting with her other lover was a very uneasy week with Lowrey. He attended to his duties, with good results, it is true, but in a very perfunctory manner. His mind was so fully occupied with his own thoughts that he was poor company, and hence was left much to himself. This made it easier for him to carry out his plan of watching over Mandy. He arranged his school hours, by beginning earlier and shortening the intermission, so as to let out half an hour earlier in the afternoon than the Snow Hill school, and thus have time to intercept Mandy.

Rose Amelia's assiduous attendance was the only hindrance to his movements. Since the interview with Mandy which Rose Amelia had seen, that small person had watched her teacher with hawk-like pertinacity. Lowrey, absorbed in his own thoughts, paid no attention to her, except to get rid of her in the evening. How to do this once for all was a puzzle to him. He thought that if he were harsher to her it might make her avoid him; but he put the thought away, for he could not be rude to any one. He finally concluded to reach the same result in another way.

"Rose Amelia," he said one afternoon when she lingered, "I don't think it looks nice for you to wait for me every evening. You are getting to be quite a large girl, and I think it would be more proper, more maidenly in every way for you to go along home with the other girls. You can talk to me at recess, and at noontime. But you had better run along home after school."

Thus plainly dismissed there was nothing for poor Rose Amelia but to outwardly submit. A week before, her submission might have been genuine, and her small heart might have found some other shrine at which to worship, or might have contented itself with an occasional smile or kind word. But, alas! she knew the motive of her teacher's conduct, and with a very human perversity, she longed for the unattainable. She had hoped to be her teacher's favorite pupil; and she saw his heart so completely filled with another that his pupils seemed like walking shadows, and his daily work a dream. And the less he noticed her, the more wildly her strangely precocious heart beat in her narrow bosom, and the more fiercely she yearned for her teacher's love. And when Lowrey, having seen her go, and thinking the coast clear set out to seek Mandy, a little black shadow moved noiselessly through the woods and followed him step by step. With a craft and patience worthy of a red Indian, she watched and waited. And henceforth no week-day trip that he made to the Lumberton Road was made without this unseen companion, whose jealousy kept growing in volume and in intensity with every meeting between the teacher and her hated rival. She hardly reached the reasoning process. She scarcely put it to herself that she was little and dark and ugly, and that Mandy was full-grown and white and beautiful. In her mind there was room for but two great dominant ideas—one that she loved her teacher, the other that he preferred another. There was a third idea, which grew, from day to day, until at last it almost overshadowed the others, and that was hatred for this white girl, who had stolen her teacher's heart. She would have loved to do her an injury.

But both Lowrey and Mandy were as utterly unconscious of Rose Amelia's surveillance, as of her love and her hatred. Several times they met and with each meeting Mandy grew kinder. She would give him no promise, but she gave him ground for hope. He had not seen her with Utley since the midnight interview, and when with Mandy he did not spend his time in disparaging his rival, but in pleading his own cause.

In the meantime Mandy was in a very disturbed frame of mind. Utley had for several days relaxed somewhat his attentions, and she did not know what to make of this, fearing that his ardor had cooled, or that she had offended him. She knew how precarious her position was, and the probable loss of the one lover gave her a deeper sense of the value of the other; and thus Utley's absence acted in two ways to further Lowrey's wishes.

Robert Utley was very busy for the two weeks preceding his wedding day. There were repairs to be made to his house; his carriage to be painted, his plantation to be looked after, his creditors to be placated, and the indispensable personal preparations to be made. And he was expected to spend every evening with Florence, whose love for him became the warmer and more absorbing as their wedding day approached—so much so, indeed, that one would wonder that she had ever been thought cold. And there was a quiet intensity about her passion of which Robert Utley was a little afraid. He had no such feeling himself, and no desire to be held up to the reciprocal requirements of such a love. He was marrying for liberty of one kind, and he did not wish to exchange one bondage for another.

Mandy's image had pursued him during the week since he had seen her, and the longer the time grew, the more eager became his wish to see her, for he was not a man accustomed to curb his desires. On Friday evening he mounted his mare and set out for the Lumberton Road, with the hope of meeting her; if he should not meet her accidentally, he meant to go boldly to her house on some pretext that would not arouse her mother's suspicion.

As luck would have it, Mandy had gone up to the plankroad on an errand for her mother, and was just turning from it into her own road when Utley espied her, and urging his horse, rode up behind her, dismounted and threw the bridle-rein over the pommel of his saddle, leaving the intelligent creature to follow him.

"Good evening, sweetheart," he said, as he overtook her.

"Are you speakin' to me, Mr. Utley?" she answered, coldly, with assumed surprise.

"Whom else should I be speaking to, darling?"

"*I'm* not yo'r darlin'. Miss Brewin'ton's yo'r darlin'. You've probably mistaken me for her."

"Don't mention that name in my presence," he said, impatiently. "I detest the very sound of it, and when it comes from your sweet lips it is more hateful still."

"You're foolin'," said Mandy, skeptically. "You're goin' to marry her Monday night, and you've got no business comin' after me when you are goin' to marry her."

"I am not married to her yet," he said. "And suppose I did, what is marriage without love? I would not be the first man, who, forced by circumstances which he could not control, has married one woman, and given his heart's best love to another. Even if I were married to that dark, ugly, cold-blooded creature, who is not fit to walk on the same ground with you, I could still love you, and give you everything you could want. You could be a lady, and have servants to wait on you, and you would be my real wife before God."

"But what would I be before other people? No, Mr. Utley, the prospec' don't attract me. But I must bid you good night. Yo'r road don't lay the same way as mine."

Meantime they had been advancing deeper into the wood, and the rapidly fading twilight had left the road in deep shadow.

Mentally cursing his companion's scruples, Utley took a new tack.

"But don't be in a hurry, Mandy. Forgive me—I was only trying you. Suppose I do not marry Florence?"

"Well?"

"I would rather ten times to one marry you."

"Well?"

"Will *you* marry me, Mandy?"

"How can I? A man can't have two wives."

"But I haven't any. 'There's many a slip 'twixt the cup and the lip.' Listen. This marriage was arranged for me by a dead woman; it has the chill of the grave on it. I would never have considered it, but I have been unfortunate, and in order to get rid of my embarrassments I have been obliged to enter on this engagement. That has smoothed my way. My engagement to a rich girl has enabled me to meet or renew obligations, to borrow money, to get on my feet, in other words. I can break it off now without utter ruin. It would make a scandal, I should be called scoundrel, I should lose caste for a while. But, darling, what would all this amount to, weighed in the balance with your love?"

He whispered this softly into Mandy's ear. He had put his arm around her waist, against but faint resistance, and had drawn her close to him. She felt his breath upon her cheek. She doubted, and yet she listened. It sounded plausible, and yet so strange, so sweet, that a gentleman, white, rich, handsome, ardent, should put himself in such a position for a poor girl such as she.

"Will you marry me, Mandy?" he said.

Through lips upon which he rained kisses, and with breath which was shortened by the pressure of his arms, she whispered, "Yes."

Then, having got his answer, Utley released her, and while he stood for a moment before her, his look of exultation gave way to one of sadness.

"But yet," he sighed, "how do I know that you will not deceive me? I give up many things—forfeit social esteem, make another woman unhappy, alienate my family and friends; and how do I know after all, that you will not fail me at the last moment? How do I know that I may trust you?"

These words, spoken with every appearance of sincerity, awoke in Mandy a vague feeling of self-reproach. She had not thought it any breach of faith to carry on with two lovers, to neither of whom she was bound, but Utley's words seemed to stamp her conduct as treacherous, or at least as light and unmaidenly.

"How can I prove it?" she said, unconsciously coming nearer to him, and looking into his eyes.

He drew her close to him. "Give me the last, best proof," he whispered. "Be mine without reserve. Then I will know that you love me, and that you will not fail me."

Then Mandy saw through his web of lies. She struggled to tear herself away from him, but he held her fast.

"Let me go," she said, "or I'll scream. I hate you and despise you."

"You shall not go," he said. "You shall not trifle with me."

He placed his hand over her mouth, and, as she struggled with him, tried to draw her deeper into the wood.

What the result would have been is uncertain. Whether she would have been strong enough to resist him successfully, or whether weapons within herself would have come to his assistance and made his victory easy, can never be known, for she was not put to the test. He had scarcely seized her, when a dark form burst from the woods, crossed the road with a spring, and pulling them apart grappled with her assailant.

Chapter 15

$\mathcal{O}$n the early morning of the following day Utley's man Primus went to the barn to attend to his master's horse. He had not put the animal up the night before, but this was no unusual circumstance for Utley was frequently away from home until late at night, in which case he would himself attend to the horse. As the man approached the barn, however, he saw Satan, saddled and bridled, standing quietly in the lane in front of the barn, and nibbling the grass and shrubs that grew in the sheltered strip nearest the fence. When the horse heard Primus approaching, he lifted his head, whinnied, and turned to the bars, against which he pressed impatiently. He had gone without his supper, and was evidently hungry.

"I wonder w'at do dis mean?" said Primus, speaking aloud, as he led the horse, tugging at the bridle, into the stable, and, removing saddle and bridle, poured a liberal measure of corn into the manger. "Whar de debbil is Mars' Bob now? In all de five years I be'n wukkin fer 'im dis is de fus' time he eber lef' his hoss out in de lane, saddled an' bridled, all night long. He must 'a' got wid a lively set er gentermen, ter git so full he couldn' put de hoss in de stable."

Primus then curried and brushed and rubbed Satan down, and having completed these functions went up the walk to the kitchen, to get his breakfast.

"W'at you reckon, Aunt 'Lish?" he said to the cook, a fat and greasy-looking woman of middle age, with a red bandana turban on her head.

"W'at I reckon 'bout w'at, Primus?" asked the cook, as she dexterously turned a flapjack.

"Jes' w'at you reckon?"

"Go 'way fum yere, you fool boy. How I gwine reckon, 'dout I got sump'n ter reckon 'bout?"

"Aunt 'Lish," said Primus with ever-increasing solemnity, "*w'at* yo' reckon?"

"I reckon you's a bawn fool, Primus McAdoo, dat's w'at I does, comin' 'roun' yere, 'sturbin' a 'oman w'en she's gittin' her breakfas'. Mars' Bob'll be yellin' heah d'reckly, and 'is brekfus' won' be ready, an' yo'll be fer ter blame."

"I doan spek you needs ter worry 'bout Mars Bob. I doan 'low he got in ve'y early las' night, an' he won' git up ve'y early."

"How does you know, laziness? You wuzn' up late 'nuff ter tell w'en Mars' Bob got home."

"No, but I foun' Satan out in de lane, saddle' an' bridle', a-neighin' an' a-whinneyin' 'cause he ain't had nuffin' ter eat."

"Dat's mighty quare," said 'Lish. "S'pos'n' you go look in Mars Bob's room an' see ef he's dere."

Primus went across the yard into the rear door of the hall, and then along the hall to the stairs. Ascending the stairs he pushed open Utley's door, which was already ajar, and looked around the room. Then he quickly retraced his steps.

"Dey ain' nobody dar, Aun' 'Lish, an' de bed ain' be'n slep' in."

"I dunno w'at ter make er dat," said the old woman. "'Tain' lack Mars Bob. Ef he had stayed in town all night he'd 'a' put up his hoss at a lib'ry stable."

"May be he drunk too much an' fell off his hoss," suggested Primus.

"G'way fum yere, you fool boy! Mars Bob done be'n a lively genterman, but he never git too drunk ter stay on a hoss. Dere's sump'n de matter, sho'. You run right ober ter Mis' Flo'ence's an' tell Miss Hannah Mars Bob ain' come home, an' Satan standin' in the yard saddle' an' bridle'. Be sho' an' doan say nuffin ter Miss Flo'ence; fer ef Mars Bob hab stayed in town all night he wouldn' want her ter know. Be keerful now, an' ef Miss Flo'ence is up an' roun' de house, manage ter git word ter Miss Hannah so Miss Flo'ence won't 'spec' nothin'. Den come back an' git yo' brekfus'."

Primus hurried across the two plantations by a well-trodden path.

Fortune favored his mission, for Miss Hannah was walking in the grove and Florence nowhere in sight. He took off his hat and ducked his head to the lady.

"Mornin', Miss Hannah."

"Good morning, Primus. Did you bring a message to me?"

"Yas'm. Aun' 'Lish tole me ter 'form you dat Mars Bob 'parted f'm de plantation yistiddy evenin' 'bout three o'clock, jest after dinner, an' ain' 'peared sence."

A shade of annoyance came into her face.

"Perhaps he stayed in town all night, at the hotel," she said. "Don't say anything about it to our servants."

"No'm. But dat ain' all. I foun' Mars Bob's hoss standin' in de yard dis mornin', saddle' an' bridle', an' de saddle was full er dirt, an' dey wuz a place in de yahd whar Satan be'n layin' down. An' he wa'n't fed las' night, fer he wuz hungry 'nuff dis mawnin' mos' fer ter chaw up de trough I put his corn in."

Mrs. Ochiltree's annoyance gave place to genuine concern as Primus was speaking. But she knew something of her nephew's habits, and was not an impulsive woman. Possibly, she thought, the near approach of his marriage had rendered him a little reckless, and that he had determined to have out his fling before he settled down to domestic life.

"Has this ever happened before?" she asked.

"No ma'm, it nebber hab. Dis is de fus' time. Mars Bob have stayed at de hotel, but he always kep' de hoss."

This put still a different face upon the matter.

"Take Satan, Primus—will he let you ride him?"

"Oh, yas'm, he'll let me an' Mars Bob ride 'im, but nobody else."

"Ride into town and inquire for him at the hotel, and then go to the Club, and find out where he was last night and when he left for home, and if you don't find him, come back and tell me personally."

Primus returned home, ate his breakfast hurriedly, and rode to town. He met several gentlemen, riding or driving, of whom he made inquiries that resulted in no definite information. One said he had ridden in town with Utley the afternoon of the day before. Another had played a game of cards with him at the Lafayette Club. But neither had seen him since.

At the hotel he had not been seen. At the Club, Primus learned that his master had been there for a couple of hours, and had gone away in the direction of his home, at about six o'clock in the afternoon.

After exhausting every source of information Primus started homeward. As he neared the plantation he met a colored man, who was walking toward town.

"Mornin', Brer Primus," said the traveler, "whar you be'n so early dis mawnin'?"

"I be'n ter town, huntin' fer Mistah Bob, ain' be'n home all night, an' ain't stayed nowhar in town."

The other negro grinned expansively.

"Nebber you mine 'bout Bob Mistah Utley. He's all right. I seen 'im walkin' wid a gal ovuh by the Lumberton Road 'bout seven o'clock las' night. De gal can prob'ly tell yer whar he stayed."

Primus bade his friend goodbye and turned into the Mineral Spring Road, a road leading to the Lumberton Plankroad, thinking he would ride around that way and seek for traces of Utley. For Primus was now almost certain there had been some accident, or else foul play, to account for his employer's disappearance.

Now, if Primus knew anything, he knew about horses, and he knew that a horse is even more a creature of habit than a man. He therefore, when he reached the Lumberton Plankroad, gave Satan free rein, confident that if he had been ridden often to any particular place, he would follow his accustomed path. The horse unhesitatingly turned to the left, and quickened his pace. When he reached the road leading to Mandy Oxendine's, which was about half a mile beyond the Mineral Spring Road, he as unhesitatingly turned into it, and kept on deeper into the forest. Finally he turned aside into a woodland path and stopped under an oak-tree, a short distance from the clearing where Mandy's cottage stood.

Primus's keen eye noted the appearance of the ground, where Satan had stood and pawed it with impatient hoofs. He saw the pendent bough, over the end of which the rein had slipped, stripping off the leaves and tender twigs. He dismounted and fastened the horse, and then took a turn in the wood, meaning, if he found nothing, to inquire at the house.

He had gone only a few rods when he came upon Utley's body. The graceful figure, which he had last seen cantering down the lane with the port of a centaur, the embodiment of proud and vigorous young manhood, now lay cold and stiff, the dead face turned toward the heaven to which it had seldom been raised in life, in the shadow of the pines through whose branches like mourning plumes the wind soughed with a dirge-like undertone.

Chapter 16

*I*n an hour after Primus's discovery of his master's body, such is the speed with which ill news is supposed always to travel, and with which it certainly traveled in this case, the fact that Utley's body had been found dead in the pinewoods was known for miles around. A coroner's jury was summoned, and an inquest was held at the scene of the murder, before the body had been removed or disturbed, for such was the law. The signs of a struggle were apparent, both in the disturbance of the surrounding ground, and in the disorder of the murdered man's clothing. And the position and depth of the fatal wound were conclusive that it was made by the hand of another, and could not have been self-inflicted. The verdict of the coroner's jury was that the deceased had come to his end by violence, at the hand of some person or persons unknown.

The body was removed to Utley's house, from which on the next day but one, the funeral took place. Florence Brewington shut herself up for a week after, and held speech with no one, not even her aunt. What agonies of grief and disappointment she endured can be imagined only by those who have seen their brightest hopes wither in the bud, who have had the sweetest cup of life dashed from their lips when but one drop has been tasted. When she resumed her place in the household, she was the same proud, cold woman as before; she kept her grief to herself, as she had so long kept her love.

The coroner's verdict as to the manner of Utley's death had of course only whetted public curiosity. Murders were of rare occurrence in Marlborough County, and the ultimate discovery of a murderer, in a sparse population, where every one knew every one else, was almost a foregone conclusion; it was only a matter of time. And the population of the county resolved itself, one might say, into a committee of the whole, to discuss and speculate upon the crime, and to unearth its perpetrator. This interest was heightened by the offer of two hundred dollars reward by the sheriff, supplemented by an offer of one hundred dollars by Miss Florence Brewington, for the discovery and arrest of the murderer.

Though Mandy had been the only witness to the tragedy in the forest, she was not the only one to fix upon Tom Lowrey as the slayer of Utley. Rose Amelia had seen her teacher at dusk on the evening of the killing, on the road leading toward Mandy's home. But a great event had taken place in her life that day, and even her interest in her teacher's movements had become a secondary consideration for the time being. Her father had served out a term in the penitentiary, to which he had been sentenced for stealing a shoat, and had returned once more to the bosom of his family. He was not a good citizen, for he had a constitutional antipathy to work, though capable of considerable mental and physical exertion in order to avoid it. With all his faults, however, he was fond of his family, and ready and willing to do anything for them except his duty. So for once Rose Amelia forsook her teacher for her father, and went home without following Lowrey farther than his path coincided with her own way homeward. But when she learned that Robert Utley had been found dead among the pines, near the Oxendine house, Rose Amelia divined at once that her teacher had met and fought and killed his rival.

Rose Amelia knew the penalty for murder. So her first impulse was to say nothing at all about the affair. She thought that she alone possessed the clue, that she alone knew of the secret meetings which had culminated in the sanguinary catastrophe, that she alone could reveal a motive sufficient to lead to the crime. She felt that by her silence she would serve her teacher, would in effect save his life. And though the secret, like a caged wild bird, beat against her narrow bosom, not for worlds would she have spoken. For when, sometime after the matter had all blown over, she should tell her teacher what she knew, would he not be bound to her by a debt of gratitude that would drive the white-faced snake from his heart? With all her shrewdness, she did not know, and never knew, that such a revelation would have made the sight of her forever hateful to him.

But Rose Amelia could not spare herself the natural enjoyment, to one of her disposition, of the possession of a weighty secret. It was a great pleasure to her to go around the settlement, and when she saw two or more people talking, to approach as near them as she could, to listen to their vague speculations, and chuckle to herself at her own superior knowledge. She, Rose 'Melia, knew more than even all the great rich white people of the county, not to mention in the same breath the ignorant colored folks, whom she had always despised because they were poor and black! For Rose Amelia's soul was that of an aristocrat, which by some wanton freak of fate had been locked up in a chrysalis from which it could never emerge; she had been heard to say that she was born white, but had been changed in her cradle. She enjoyed the pleasure of self-congratulation on her superior knowledge for one day only; for on the second day, to her great alarm, she heard the nearness of Mandy's house to the scene of the murder commented upon, and learned that others besides herself had seen Utley in company with the girl.

It needed but a spark to fire a train of ideas in Rose Amelia's mind, naturally precocious in some directions, and now doubly sharpened by the sense of her teacher's peril. If, she reasoned, the crime could be fixed upon this white girl, her teacher would be saved even from suspicion, and her rival effectually removed and adequately punished. There was a sufficient touch of ancestral savagery in the child to make even such a fearful reprisal as that of the gallows almost as sweet to her as the knowledge of her teacher's safety. She would denounce Mandy as the murderess, and would detail circumstances sufficient to demonstrate her guilt.

But while Rose Amelia could conceive the main idea, she could not work out the details of her plan. She could never have plucked up courage enough to go herself to the officers and accuse Mandy of the crime. But she thought of a substitute more familiar with the law and its methods. She perceived in her unworthy parent an instrument ready to her hand. She had a confidence in his baseness abundantly justified by her knowledge of his past; and she credited him with a cunning hardly borne out by his record, for he had been detected more than once in his breaches of the law. But his cupidity was beyond question, and she could safely rely upon the offered reward as a sufficient incentive to anything that might place it within his reach. Three hundred dollars was a fortune to a man like Gab'l Sunday, and would mean an unlimited quantity of guzzling and swilling and diversified debauchery. Rose Amelia did not take her father entirely into her confidence, but merely told him that she had seen Robert Utley go into the woods with Mandy Oxendine on the evening of the murder, and that she had seen them together more than once before, and that as the murder had taken place near her house, she had probably committed it.

Gabriel Sunday caught eagerly at the suggestion, and spared Rose any further trouble. It was an emergency that brought out the dormant powers of the ex-convict, whose fame as a liar was even greater than his reputation as a thief. He went next day to the sheriff and told him that his daughter had seen Utley and Mandy enter the woods, and had heard angry words pass between them; that the woman had demanded that Utley marry her, and had threatened to kill him if he did not. To this plausible story he added several circumstantial details that harmonized with the main composition, and which he relied upon Rose Amelia to confirm when he had reported them to her.

This information was from such a doubtful source that unsupported by other facts it would not have received much credit. But there had been a growing feeling in the community, due to Utley's well-known character, that a woman was at the bottom of the affair, and that the woman must be sought and found before the mystery could be solved. Gabriel Sunday's information fitted in with this theory. It also led to a more careful search of the ground near where the body was found, and to the discovery, on a neighboring bush, of a torn bit of cloth from a woman's gown. While neither the story nor this discovery nor the nearness of Mandy's home to the scene of the crime, were conclusive of her guilt, they furnished such ground for suspicion that a warrant for her arrest was sworn out, and two constables sent to execute it.

Chapter 17

*M*eantime, what of Mandy?

On that dreadful night, too frightened to move and scarcely able to breathe, she had stood for a minute or two—it seemed to her like an hour—watching the two men struggling in the obscurity of the night and the deep shadows combined. Suddenly they had fallen, and after continuing the struggle on the ground for a moment, the uppermost of the two had relaxed his hold and with a groan rolled over to one side. The victor had sprung to his feet and without a word had vanished into the forest as quickly as he had come.

By this time the full horror of the situation had burst upon Mandy, and she had turned and fled. She had not been able to distinguish the faces of the two men during the struggle, but she knew that the one in the light coat, left lying there under the pines, was the man whose kiss had but the moment before been pressed upon her lips. She had not recognized the face of her rescuer—she had no wish to see it, for she preferred not to know who he was, though in her heart she had no doubt of his identity. It was, up to this time, the most tragic moment of her life, into which experiences were crowding rapidly. One of the two men who had loved her most lay dead in the woods—for some instinct told her that a mortal blow had been struck—dead by the hand of the other, himself now a criminal, outlawed from life and love. And she felt herself the not altogether innocent cause of a catastrophe which, with all its other horrors, involved the destruction of her own aims and hopes.

She had not slept during the night, and scarcely stirred from the house for the next two days. When she had first heard of the murder from a neighbor who came to tell of it, she had tried to exhibit just the ordinary surprise and curiosity that such an event would arouse in one not personally interested; and she had played her part so well, that not even her mother observed anything unusual in her speech or manner.

When the officers sent to arrest her entered the house she divined that their errand was in connection with the Utley affair and turned to them a pale face filled with vague alarm.

"Is yo' name Amanda Oxendine?" asked one of the men.

"Yes, that's my name," she answered.

"We've got a warrant fer yer," said the spokesman.

"What for?" she asked, with white lips.

"Fer killin' Bob Utley."

"But I didn't kill him," she said, with indignant vehemence. Then in a moment all her vital forces seemed to desert her, and she would have fallen if one of the men had not caught her and placed her in the chair from which she had risen.

Her conduct was entirely natural. The idea that she would be arrested had never occurred to her, and her evident indignation was not only consistent with her innocence, but what might have been expected of her under the circumstances. At the same instant, however, the possible consequences flashed across her mind, and she realized the impotence even of her innocence to save her from things, to a sensitive person, but one degree less terrible than death. But the officers did not possess her knowledge nor her sensitiveness, and so they thought her manner damning evidence of guilt.

"I wouldn' have nothin' mo' ter say, ef I wuz you," said the other constable, "fer whatever you say is liable ter be used ag'in you; we 'uns 'ud hafter swear to it, fer that's the law. I wouldn' open my mouth, ef I wuz you, ontel I saw a lawyer. But we'll read the warrant to you."

Mandy recovered herself in a few moments, and sat like a statue while they read the warrant, scarcely hearing more than a confused jumble of sounds. Her mother did not seem as much distressed as Mandy. She kept her seat in the chimney-corner, and rocked herself to and fro on her chair. She had been carding cotton, and still moved the cards mechanically back and forth.

"I tol' you they wuz bad luck comin' ter this house," she croaked. "I knowed it when you broke that lookin'-glass. It's a sign that never fails. An' the trouble is jus' begun, chile."

"You'd better quit prophesyin' evil, ole 'oman," said one of the constables, "an' get up an' get some clothes an' things together fer the gal. She'll prob'bly need 'em befo' she gets home again."

The old woman made up a bundle of clothes for Mandy, and kissed her mechanically. Then Mandy went out with the officers and got into the buggy that stood waiting to convey her to jail. The old woman stood in the doorway watching the buggy until it was hidden by the trees. When she could not longer see her daughter a full comprehension of the situation seemed to dawn upon her mind, and breaking into the wail of an old person in whom the fountain of tears is well-nigh dry, she turned and went into her cabin.

*T*hey drove along the main road to Rosinville. The officers had been reticent about their errand to Sandy Run, lest the accused might be warned of her danger and seek safety in flight. But the secret had leaked out, and it seemed as though the whole population had turned out to see the murderess taken to jail. At every gate, at every roadside cabin door, by every well or watering trough, the country people were gathered. There were men and women, boys and girls, all gazing curiously at the rare spectacle of a woman who had killed a man. And fond mothers, anxious that their offspring should lose no proper pleasure, held up their nursing infants, that they might see the murderess pass by, and be able in after years to recount the event among the memorable occurrences of their lives.

Mandy fixed her eyes straight before her, and set her face like a flint. What right, she thought indignantly, had these people to be gazing at her? She had done no wrong. Her outraged innocence protested against this unmerited punishment. She did not know that though the law presumes an accused innocent until his guilt is proved, public opinion treats him as guilty until the law has spoken.

When they entered the town the crowds were larger, but of a somewhat different make-up. As they went through the main street, merchant and clerk, lawyer and client, doctor and patient, came to the street doors to gaze upon the young and handsome woman who had been arrested for murder. The constables who had her in charge were not men of sentiment, and made no effort to shield her; indeed, they felt their office magnified by this display of public interest. They drove slowly, the officers nodding familiarly to such acquaintances as they passed on the street. They even stopped at a well in the town to water the horse, thus giving the curious an opportunity to scrutinize the prisoner more closely.

But, while Mandy for a while felt keenly the humiliation to which she was subjected, after the first spasm of shame other thoughts took possession of her mind—thoughts which so absorbed her faculties as to render her oblivious of and therefore indifferent to what was going on around her. She was innocent of the actual crime; her hand had not struck the fatal blow. But was she not guilty before God? Had not this tragedy been the outcome of her own folly, her own lightness, her own wickedness? If so, was it not right that her life should pay the forfeit?

But there was more involved in the situation than her own life, or the mere punishment of a crime. The life of one she loved was in danger. For not until the murder had she realized how deeply, how passionately, how completely she loved Lowrey. There seemed to come back to her, in a great surge of feeling, the passion of two years before, when her heart first woke to love, when Tom was all the world to her, and father and mother, home and friends, duty, virtue—everything—would have seemed but dim phantoms, to be swept away as with a breath, if they had stood between her and her love.

The primitive woman loved the lover who for love had slain his rival, and there was something of the primitive woman in Mandy's nature, as there is revealed in every woman's, when, in times of strong passion or intense excitement, the veil of modernity is for a moment lifted. Her true lover had slain the false one for love of her; for love of her he had forfeited his life. There was but one sure way to pay the debt. If she, who had not committed the crime, had been arrested, what hope of ultimate escape was there for the guilty, if she should go clear? He had forfeited his life for her; could she do less for him? In her present exalted state of mind life without him seemed not worth living. Life with him was now an impossible dream. Of what use to her in any event would be her life? She could not hope to conceal her antecedents longer, and she would not have cared to return to her old life. She made a grand resolve.

When they reached the jail, and Mandy was helped down from the buggy by her captors, the sheriff met them at the door. He seemed a not unkindly man, and gentler in manner than might be expected from his office, though perhaps the youth and beauty of his prisoner were not without their effect upon him.

"I'm sorry," he said, "to see you in such a fix. I hope you'll be able to prove your innocence."

"I can't," she said. "I am guilty; I am the murderer."

"Be careful what you say," he said, "for it may be used against you. You are excited now and not responsible for what you are saying."

"I know perfectly well what I am sayin', an' I mean it. In the sight of God I am responsible for the murder of Robert Utley."

The sheriff said no more, but, accompanied by the jailer, who stood by with his keys in hand, consigned the prisoner to one of the cells reserved for female offenders.

As Mandy was a woman and white, some effort was made to render her more comfortable than ordinary prisoners could expect in Marlborough County jail. Instead of a blanket on the bare floor, she was furnished with a straw mattress, a table and a chair, and while she remained in prison her food was supplied from the jailer's own table.

She passed the night wretchedly. For hours she lay awake in her dismal cell, tortured by thoughts which banished sleep. But towards morning tired nature and perfect health reasserted their claims, and she fell into a doze, which, troubled now and then by dreams, lasted until the noise of a dog barking in the jail-yard aroused her. She rose, washed her face in the tin basin with which the cell was provided, and smoothed her hair as best she could with her hands. There was no comb in the cell. She had completed this simple toilet and had put her mattress in order, when the key turned in the lock, the door of her cell opened, and the jailer came in with her breakfast.

He seemed inclined to conversation, but she answered his questions briefly, and when he had asked how she slept, and whether he could do anything else for her comfort, and had suggested that it was going to be a warm day, he lingered yet a moment, but finding that she was not in a mood for conversation he went away. She heard the muffled sound of voices as he conversed with several of the other prisoners, and then the click of the lock, the harsh grating of the outer door that shut her out from liberty, from love, from hope. True, she might open it by speaking, but only to see it close on Tom Lowrey, as she passed out.

In the dark hours of the night black dreams had come to her, and the terror of death had fallen upon her. She had once been taken, when a child, to see a man hanged for burglary, under the humane code of North Carolina. She recalled with the vividness of reality every event of that day: the old field, overgrown with weeds, and here and there a solitary persimmon tree or a short-leafed pine; the rude gallows, with the dangling noose; the surging crowd, not noisy and bandying ribald jests, but speaking in low tones and with solemn inflections; the death-cart, on which the condemned man sat between two jailers; the minister's prayer; the pinioning of the condemned man's arms, the black cap; the agony of suspense, the fatal drop, the thrill of horror, the black burden of the gallows swinging to and fro; the groans, the shudders, the sobs of hysterical women. She remembered how she had turned and run, far, far away from the scene of this judicial murder, and how for a week she had been afraid of the dark, had been frightened at shadows, and how slowly her mind had shaken off these dark impressions. And in the night she had almost wavered in her purpose, the sacrifice had seemed almost too great. But with daylight and food and drink the shadows departed. She felt stronger and more capable of carrying out her purpose.

Chapter 18

About nine o'clock Mandy heard the key grate again in the prison lock and the outer door creak dismally on its hinges. The heavy tread of the jailer mounted the stairs, accompanied by a lighter footstep. The jailer paused at her cell, unlocked the door, and threw it open.

"A visitor fer you," he said. "I don't know the elder personally, but I've heard of him, and as he says you're one of his flock, I've let 'im in. It's a privilege that we allow preachers an' near relation; all others have to get passes."

Again Mandy felt the mingled attraction and repulsion which always came over her in the presence of Elder Gadson, for it was he who stood before her. But after a moment, as she looked at him more closely, the feeling of repulsion became the stronger of the two, and she shivered with an indefinable impulse of fear. It was Elder Gadson, it is true, but not as she last had seen him. Then he had stood in the pulpit, his eyes streaming with tears, his hands upstretched to God, almost a halo surrounding his head. And now she looked upon a face torn with passion, upon eyes that flamed, upon lips cracked and parched and red where he had bit them in his agony. The priest had been stripped off like a husk, and the man beneath him stood revealed. He had tried to be calm when he spoke to the turnkey. But now that that official had locked them up together and turned discreetly to another part of the jail, Elder Gadson's soul looked out from his face, and the intensity of his feeling seemed to scorch Mandy like a hot wind, even before he had opened his mouth.

"I did not think to ever see you in such a place," he said. His voice sounded hoarse and strange, and Mandy shrank from him still more when she heard it.

"We never know where our sins will bring us," she answered with an effort.

"It was another's sin that brought you here," he said.

"It was my own. I was too proud to be what God made me, too vain to be content with my lot. I didn't act right, an' my punishment is just."

"He wuz his own murderer," said the preacher. "He carved out his own fate. It wuz the jedgment of God, and a human hand wuz the pore instrument to carry it out. When God wuz angry with the Egyptians he did not smite them with his own hand, but sent his angels to slay their first-born."

He spoke eagerly, passionately. Mandy wondered at the intensity of his feeling.

"But, why," he said, "have you let yo'rself be locked up fer this murder? It wuz not yo'r hand that struck the blow. Why didn't you tell the name of the man that killed him?"

"I killed him," she said. "His death lies at my door."

The preacher seemed puzzled for a moment. Then a glad look brightened his face, as though he were experiencing a great and un-hoped for joy.

"Ah," he said, "you make me happy beyond compare. But it ain't worth while for you to die. Fly with me! I can get you out, and we will go away, far away, to another state, and be happy! Say you will come with me, darlin'!"

He leaned over toward her, his eyes burning with passion. She sprang back as he drew nearer to her, and put up her hand instinctively, as though to ward off some hateful or harmful thing. Even the mistaken idea that the preacher had formed could not make him misread the look upon her face. His joy vanished, his face grew dark, and sadness, mingled with wonder, sat upon his brow.

"You do not love me, then?" he asked.

"No," she said, "I don't love you. What have I ever said or done to make you think I love you? I am not for the love of any man. I am the bride of death. The gallows will be my altar, and a shroud my bridal robe."

"No, no," he said, and he spoke with more restraint, for he had learned something in this interview that he had not known before. "Not so. You do not need to die. Whatever be your motive in shieldin' the murderer of Robert Utley, I cannot believe it was your hand that cut short his evil life, that stilled his treach'rous heart. You have chosen to take the burden on yourself, and to shield him from punishment for what, perhaps, was not a crime before God. Perhaps he slew the other in self-defense, perhaps he broke one law to prevent him from transgressin' a higher law. You choose to shield him. But is it necessary to do so at the cost of your own life?"

"You do not seem to understand," said Mandy, "that I and I alone killed Robert Utley, and I alone should pay the penalty."

"I hear you; and if you did kill him, what then? Need you add one more to the number of the dead? Fly with me, and far from this place, you will have time to repent, time to atone for all the evil you have done. Remain, and the shadow of the gallows will darken your future, yes, may even shut out the light of God's face, and you may go down to the grave in darkness of soul. Be mine," he said, eagerly, fiercely, seizing her hand, which he gripped unconsciously so hard that she could scarce keep from screaming with pain. "Be my wife, my companion, my solace, and to-gether we will ask pardon for our sins; for Christ who gave himself for us, can make even the vilest clean."

She shivered, and tore loose her hand. "I cannot," she said. "I do not love you. Life with you would be a livin' death."

"Do not say so," he pleaded eagerly, almost despairingly. They heard the footsteps of the jailer returning. "Reflec'. Think of your life, your youth, your beauty. Think what a world of happiness may be yours. I will love you more than any other man could love you. To me there is but one woman in the world. I will wrap you in a mantle of love as wide as the earth. Goodbye," he said, as he kissed her with his eyes, which seemed to burn into her face. "Goodbye, my sister"—struggling to re-sume his professional manner as the jailer stood waiting—"when I come again to-morrow I hope to find you more disposed to listen to the words of the Lord, and repent while yet there is time to turn and flee from the divine wrath."

The door clanged to behind them, and Mandy was left alone, with another thread added to the tangled web of her life. This man, too, loved her, and was willing to give up his work, to leave his home, to break the law, and lead the life of a hunted fugitive for her sake. But not only did she not love him; she loved Tom Lowrey, and, in her present state of mind, the thought of another man would have been the blackest treachery. Besides, there seemed something like profanation in the offer of love from this man, whom she had associated only with the higher needs of the soul. She had no notions or views concerning the celibacy of the priesthood; she did not know there was a celibate priesthood. There was no Catholic church where she had lived; only the narrowest Protestant sectarianism had prevailed. The men who had served the churches in her vicinity had been plain men, who lived with their families, and rose above their neighbors only by virtue of their office. But in Elder Gadson Mandy had from the first perceived a power, that acted upon her as a disturbing influence, from the moment she had first drawn his notice. If the influence had been altogether an attractive one, he could have led her, she felt, to the end of the world. But it had been repellant, and the repulsion had grown stronger with the development of her love for Lowrey. The idea of love in connection with him seemed a sort of sacrilege—like dancing in a church, or playing cards on Sunday, or any other deadly form of sin recognized by the simple creed of the Hardshell Baptists. She could not think of it without a shudder.

Chapter 19

*R*ose Amelia had expected, after Mandy Oxendine's arrest, to see the face of her teacher show the relief he must feel at his own security. On the contrary, during the whole of the Friday following the arrest Lowrey had been the visible prey of the most violent agitation. He had gone through his duties mechanically, and by his unusual manner had attracted the attention of all his pupils. He did not speak a word to Rose Amelia during the day, except in the course of recitations, and it was evident to the dullest pupil that something was wrong with the teacher.

Lowrey was of a reflective turn of mind. After the first shock of the news he began to consider the situation, and to weigh the probabilities. First, Mandy had already been arrested, had already suffered a large part of the disgrace and ignominy. His heart overflowed with sympathy as he thought of it, but he did not let his feelings interrupt his argument. Second, being a woman, it was altogether likely that Mandy would have a trial, and being a young and beautiful woman, that she would have a fair trial, and in the absence of anything but circumstantial evidence, that she would, if defended by a skillful lawyer, stand a fair chance of acquittal. The mere fact of the arrest of a young and handsome woman for murder would suggest either self-defense or revenge for slighted love, and no jury would be likely to convict a white woman for either offense. Again, with himself on the outside, studying, as well as his position would allow, the popular feeling, if there should seem any doubt of her acquittal, he might by skill and daring, effect her escape from prison. So that from any point of view she had a fair chance to go clear of punishment. He had collected a part of his salary as teacher, and the remainder would be due in a week. With this he could employ counsel to defend her, and have money, if need be, to procure means of escape.

But before deciding upon anything, it was necessary to see Mandy. He dismissed his school at three o'clock, and hurrying to the town, presented himself at the jail and asked to see Mandy Oxendine.

"Air you her brother?" asked the jailer.

"No," he said.

"Then you kya'nt git in without a' order f'm the sheriff. You'll find 'im at his office up on Front Street. Nobody but members of a prisoner's fam'ly er preachers is 'lowed to visit pris'ners without a' order."

Lowrey hastened toward the sheriff's office. But as he neared it his pace slackened. Several reflections occurred to him. He was known to the sheriff, for that officer had countersigned his voucher, and he had talked to him about the Sandy Run School. If he should be asked the reason of his interest in Mandy, what could he say? Not the truth, of course. He could not claim to be a relative, for she was white, and no explanation could get over that difficulty; and if the fact of Mandy's blood should be declared, it would undoubtedly spoil the effect of her youth and beauty, for then the sleeping dogs of race hatred would be stirred up, and one could predict the result with reasonable certainty. Perhaps it would be better to communicate with her in some other way, through her mother perhaps, as she was the only person who knew of his relations with Mandy.

He had not fully made up his mind however, when he reached the sheriff's office. This was a small frame building, painted white, with a piazza extending across the front. A row of splint-bottomed chairs were set against the wall, and afforded convenient seats for loungers. In fact the sheriff's office was a favorite loafing-place for politicians, small officials, and men about town. As Lowrey drew near he saw that several of the seats were occupied. The men were engaged in animated conversation, and from the first words he learned that their theme was the murder of Robert Utley. Lowrey was eager to know what they said, so he sauntered up on the porch, and stood apparently reading the placards posted on the wall—notices of sheriff's sales, of administrator's sales, of appraisements, and among them the notice offering a reward for the apprehension of Utley's murderer.

"She's a mighty likely gal," said one of the group. "A fellow would almost risk the chance of bein' killed to be on good terms with her."

"Bob Utley always did have luck with the women," said another. "I remember—" and he went off into a story in which Utley figured as the principal character, and played a despicable role. The story, however, seemed to be greatly enjoyed by the group, who laughed immoderately.

"I wouldn' mind being jailer till court opens," said another of the party, whom Lowrey had once had pointed out to him as a "man who had killed his nigger." "Reckon I'll go over an' offer to keep jail fer Bill while he takes a vacation."

"Bill air no fool," said a third, a long-haired individual, in a voice somewhat impeded by a huge quid of tobacco. "Bill takes good keer ter collect the perq'isites er his office."

This sally was greeted with a horse-laugh that echoed through the neighborhood, brought several people to windows across the street to look inquiringly out, and woke a dog slumbering in the sunlight and set him to barking loudly at an imaginary adversary. It also sent a red flood to Lowrey's face.

"I remember," said the second speaker, "when Cicely Murchison wuz in jail fer shootin' Tom Miller—that wuz ten years ago. *She* wuz a fine lookin' woman. The sheriff thought so, the jailer thought so too, the prosecutin' attorney was of the same opinion. *She* got good treatment in jail, and wuz acquitted without the jury leavin' the box. Bill wuz jailer then, an' yer can't break an old dog from suckin' aigs. Yer see—"

He went on for a few minutes in a strain that left no doubt as to his meaning. Lowrey could scarce contain himself, and at length, when he could bear no more sprang down from the piazza with flushed cheeks, anger alternating in his bosom with jealous fear. God help Mandy if such were the hands to which she must be confided for the six weeks intervening before the opening of court!

People looked at Lowrey in astonishment as he rushed along the street with set face and clenched fists. The jail was the magnet that drew him, and in the woods around it he wandered until late in the afternoon, a prey to the frightful visions conjured up by the coarse and heartless merriment of the group on the sheriff's piazza. What chance had she to defend herself against violence? Solitude, hunger, darkness, chains—any kind of cruelty might be brought to bear upon her. And what weapons had she to defend herself? Her pride cast down, her self-respect destroyed—with nothing left but life and honor, would she be able to defend the latter if the former were threatened? Her mother was poor. He himself could not come forward as her champion, and if he could have done so, he was himself poor and of the despised caste. Alas, poor Mandy! She seemed destined to pay dear for her fatal beauty.

In the light of this new idea, all other considerations faded into insignificance. In the fierce tumult of love and jealousy that had sprung up in Lowrey's heart, he would rather have seen her dead than dishonored, and a thousand times dead rather than become the burden of ribald jests and vulgar merriment.

He saw but one certain way to rescue her from this impending fate. When a possible acquittal after the lapse of a few weeks or months was the question, reason, prudence, foresight, a thousand springs might be permitted to control his conduct. But with dishonor imminent, there was but one way in which to save her from it, and that way required prompt and decisive action. The only way to secure her release was for him to take her place. The chances were against his escaping the extreme penalty of the law, but if he must die, she would at least be free and happy. She could be happy without him, but without her he did not care for life.

Having made up his mind to this course, he turned and walked rapidly back to the town. By this time the sun had set and the loafers on the sheriff's piazza were just getting up, preparatory to going home to supper. The sheriff himself had just put the key in the lock to close the office when a man stepped up behind him and said, in hoarse accents:

"I wish to give myself up."

The sheriff sprang back startled.

"Who in the devil are you?" he asked, not recognizing Lowrey in the gathering dusk. Indeed, he had only seen him once or twice before, though he had heard the young teacher spoken of as a smart fellow.

"My name is Thomas Lowrey, teacher of the Sandy Run Colored School."

"And for God's sake, Lowrey," exclaimed the sheriff with genuine surprise, "what do you want to give yourself up for?"

"For the killing of Robert Utley."

Chapter 20

*W*hen Elder Gadson left the jail he had gone straight through the town and out to the house on the sandhills where he made his temporary home. The people of the house were away, but he knew where the key was kept, and securing it, procured food and drink. He then returned the key to its hiding-place, and went out into the woods, mainly to avoid meeting any of the church people who might call to see him. He wanted to be alone; he was in no mood for conversation. The image of Mandy, her danger, his powerlessness to aid her, filled his mind to the exclusion of all other subjects. These thoughts, and one other, which weighed still more heavily, made up a burden almost too great for a mind already half-crazed by passion. For hours he wandered distractedly among the pines, and at midnight crept homeward, and threw himself upon his bed. He caught but a few hours of restless sleep, troubled by horrible dreams, and ere the gray morning had barely dawned he was awake. At breakfast, in answer to inquiries from his hostess, he accounted, in a somewhat incoherent way, for his late absence the night before. He could not eat, but drank several cups of strong coffee to steady his nerves.

He was going to visit Mandy again, and make another effort to get her to listen to reason. Surely she must be touched by his appeals; surely she must yield to such a love as his. All the pent-up passion of his life of abstinence was poured out upon this weak girl, whose brown hair had bewitched him, who had driven his religion from the altar of his heart and installed in its place the twin devils of jealousy and desire.

He could not wait until a suitable hour to call at the jail, but started out for it shortly after sunrise. He made a long detour, going around the town and entering it at the opposite side, near the jail. By this means he occupied the time until the prisoner could be visited; he also avoided meeting other people, and therefore did not learn that another prisoner had been thrown into jail the evening before for the same crime with which Mandy was charged.

At about nine o'clock Elder Gadson knocked at the door of the jail. The jailer answered the summons. He was surly and suspicious. He had visited Mandy's cell several times, carrying up her meals, and finding other pretexts to speak to her. Certain plans he had formed were not going as well as he wished, and it was necessary to their successful operation that Mandy Oxendine should not see too many people.

"I'll go," he said, "and see if she wants you let in."

He went up-stairs with a great clatter of footsteps, and soon returned.

"She says she don't keer to see any preacher to-day. She's got a headache and don't want to be disturbed."

Elder Gadson showed a five-dollar note—one of the few that he possessed. The jailer's eyes glistened covetously, and he instinctively started to put out his hand. But he did not complete the gesture. He would not let this black-coated preacher spoil his plans by too much preaching.

"I'm astonished," he said coldly, "that you sh'd attemp' ter corrup' a' officer o' the law. Money, suh, is wuth much, but duty mo'. I shall be compelled, suh, to request you not ter come here any mo', an' you kin be thankful ef I don't repo't you ter the proper authorities. When the prisoner asks for a preacher I'll sen' fer one."

He slammed the door in the elder's face, and its clang sounded the death-knell of the elder's hopes. With communication cut off he could no longer hope to induce her to fall in with his plans. He was not a man of the world, and his life had run along in one narrow channel. He knew little about courts, or juries, or the technicalities of the law. To him an arrest seemed almost synonymous with a conviction, and the Old Testament injunction: "Whoso sheddeth a man's blood, by men shall his blood be shed," carried with it the weight of the divine sanction. He was not of the type of preachers who spend their lives in explaining away the

Scriptures, but was of the school which read and believed them literally. Perhaps it is a misnomer to call the simple faith of the elder's followers a "school" of thought or belief. Their religion was a tradition; they accepted its current teachings as they did the course of the seasons, and thought no more of disputing the one than the other.

All day long this text remained uppermost in the wretched man's mind: "Whoso sheddeth a man's blood, by men shall his blood be shed." And in his wild imaginings he seemed to see a sea of blood spreading wide before him, and on the crimson tide a white face floating. And on the verge he saw himself standing, stretching out his hand in vain, and in imminent danger of himself falling into the flood.

"I must speak to her," he groaned. "She must listen. I will wait until dark, and then I will get to the window of her cell and compel her to listen."

All day long he waited, without food, but drinking deeply and often from some creek or spring, for fiery passions consumed him.

When night had fallen he turned his footsteps toward the jail. He kept out of sight among the trees until he had reached the side farthest from the jailer's house, that being the side on which Mandy's cell was located. There was a picket-fence around the jail-yard, but it was not so high but that a determined man could scale it. He began to climb the fence, making as little noise as possible, and had just reached the top and was preparing to jump down on the other side, when there was a swift rush, a low growl. In a moment the growl became a deep bay, and by the light of the rising moon, he saw the huge form of a bloodhound awaiting his descent.

He had not anticipated this obstacle. He was provided with no weapon, and the dog was a powerful one. He recalled now that he had seen the dog quietly asleep in the jail-yard on the day of his visit to Mandy, and he remembered too that he had heard of the viciousness and keen scent of the beast. He climbed down quickly, and moved away as quietly and rapidly as he could.

It was necessary to meet this new condition. He thought of poisoning the dog; but he could not procure poison that night, and he must speak to Mandy; he felt as though he could not live another day unless he spoke to her. If properly armed, he surely ought to be able to silence a dog. He walked off down the road to search for a suitable weapon. There was a bit of woods between the jail and the town, and here he hoped to find a club which would answer his purpose.

He had nearly covered the cleared space between the jail and the wood, when he heard the tramp of footsteps approaching from the town. He quickened his pace, as he did not wish to be seen. He had almost reached the shelter of the trees when he came face to face with a party of about a dozen men, all on foot, some armed with guns and others unarmed. He shrank to one side of the road, but it was not dark enough to prevent his being seen by several of the party. They did not speak, however, but moved rapidly and quietly towards the jail, intent upon their own purposes.

The preacher did not know what to think of this meeting, and he stood for a moment in doubt whether to turn and follow the party or to continue his search for a weapon. Before he had reached a decision, he heard other footsteps drawing near, and not wishing to be seen he sprang forward into the chaparral as another and larger party of men went by to join the first. Elder Gadson stood listening intently and looking to see if others would pass. Presently, coming from the direction of the town, he saw a small figure creeping swiftly and silently along the side of the road that lay in the deepest shadow. He could not make out whether this solitary figure was that of a man or a woman, but, observing it closely at a certain spot where the trees had been cut away from the roadside, the face was silhouetted against the sky, and he saw that it was the face of a little negro girl.

Chapter 21

The errand of the party that had gone to the jail was an unusual one for Marlborough County. The relations of the two races which make up the population of North Carolina had always been more friendly than in most Southern States, and in Marlborough County more harmonious even than in other parts of the State. The life of a negro was as a rule held as sacred as that of a white man, and every man accused of a crime had been given, generally speaking, at least the semblance of a fair trial.

But the times were slightly troubled. A political contest was impending. The two great political parties were more evenly balanced in North Carolina than in most Southern States, both in the number and the quality of their supporters, and there was a kind of feeling in the air that danger threatened the supremacy of the party in power. The color line had been drawn with its unusual strictness, and considerations of right and justice had lost something of their clearness in the heat of partisan politics. So that when, on the afternoon of the day following Tom Lowrey's incarceration, some one of a little knot of men on Front Street suggested that a Negro who had killed a white man ought not to be allowed to live any longer than it would take to kill him, the remark was not received with disfavor. The lynching fever which has since swept over the South and disgraced the nation, had at that time not yet broken out, but the memory of the Ku Klux Klan was still green, and elsewhere in the South there were plenty of precedents both for the act and for a probable immunity from punishment therefor.

There was some demurring at first to the proposition. But there was in the party a young man who had long been an ardent admirer of Florence Brewington. Though Sandy McAllister, as this young man was called, had never received the slightest encouragement at Miss Brewington's hands, he had often thought that with Utley out of the way he might have a chance to win her affections. One would have expected this ardent lover to feel rather grateful than otherwise to the man who had removed his rival. But when the question of lynching Lowrey was broached, it occurred to McAllister that by a conspicuous activity in revenging Utley's murder he might win the gratitude of her who was to have been Utley's bride, and thus advance his own suit. Hence he eagerly advocated the proposed lynching, and bore down all opposition, with the result that after dark a party had rendezvoused in the heart of the town and marched out toward the jail under his leadership.

When the mob reached the gate that led into the jail-yard they found it locked. Several of the party then went up to the jailer's house, in the adjoining yard, and knocked loudly at the door.

"Who's there?" came back the jailer's voice.

"Somebody that wants to see you, an' wants to see you bad."

"Come in the mornin'. I've gone to bed."

"Ye'll haf ter git up. We must see you. We've got a prisoner for you to lock up."

Now, jailers are paid in proportion to the number of their prisoners, and after some grumbling and swearing, the door was opened and the jailer appeared in the doorway.

"Whar's the prisoner?" he demanded.

"That was a mistake, Bill," said McAllister. "We want a prisoner. We are goin' ter lynch the murderer of Bob Utley."

"Which one of 'em?" said the jailer. "I've got two."

"The nigger Lowrey. Hurry up an' let us in the jail. We mean business an' we don't want no foolin'. "

"Now, look here, boys," said the jailer, "this kind o' thing ain't goin' to do. The prisoners in this here jail is put in my han's for safe keepin', an' I'm responsible to the sheriff for 'em, an' I'm goin' ter do my dooty."

"Come, hurry up, Bill, hand out the keys," said another. "We 'uns knows all about yer dooty. We're goin' ter do *our* dooty, an' that's ter hang the nigger. We pay taxes, we does, an' I don't want to pay fer tryin' no nigger fer murder. Hand over the keys."

"Gentlemen," said the jailer, in a milder tone, "I'll defend the prisoner at the risk er my life; that is—" he added, "unless violence is resorted to ter prevent me. As long as these arms is free, I'll do my dooty."

One of the mob stuck the muzzle of a gun in his face with a grin, while another tied his hands behind with a handkerchief.

"Gentlemen," he said, "I can't answer such an argyment. I can't resist if I ain't allowed to."

"Now, hand out the keys, Bill, like a good fellow."

"I couldn't give up them keys consistently with my dooty. I wouldn't even tell where they air, unless my life was threatened."

"Bill," said one, "tell us where the keys are or we'll blow yer brains out."

"Gentlemen, I purtest agin' this outrage. Nothin' shell injuce me to tell you whereabouts in the cupboard in my settin'-room I keeps the jail keys."

The keys were secured, and in a moment the gate to the jail-yard was unlocked. Sandy McAllister started through first, but was confronted by the bloodhound and hastily retreated.

"Kill the dog," cried several of the more impatient; "put a ball through him."

"Oh, no," said another, "he's a good dog. We didn't come to kill a good dog, but a bad nigger."

"That dog's wuth two good niggers," said another. "We'll call Bill."

The jailer came very quickly when he heard that the dog was in danger, and called him off. When he had been secured in his kennel, the jail-doors were unlocked. Lowrey's cell was entered, and he was seized and led down stairs. He did not resist, for he saw the folly of resistance. He could scarcely deny his guilt, for he had already admitted it. In fact, the fate confronting him was what he had known he must anticipate, but he had scarcely expected it so soon, or in so unceremonious a fashion.

They led him out of the jail-yard and down the road to the woods where Elder Gadson had disappeared a quarter of an hour before. Going a short distance into the woods, to a point where a large oak tree stood alone in the center of a small clearing, they halted under its shadow. Jeff Skinner, a withered relic of ante-bellum times, produced a rope, in which a noose had already been made, passed the noose over Lowrey's head, and threw the other end across a limb of the tree. Skinner had been a slave-driver in the palmy days before the war, and he scented the blood of a negro with the zest of a long dormant but re-awakened appetite.

"Air we all ready?" said the volunteer hangman.

"Hol' on a minute, Jeff," said Dan Peebles, who had once been a justice of the peace. "Don't be in sech a hurry. This here ain't no hoss-race, but a solem' expression o' public opinion. Let's do it decently an' in order. Ef the nigger's got anything ter say, he ought ter be 'lowed ter say it. He's confessed his crime, but there's a white woman in jail charged with the same killin'. He can't clear himself but he may help the woman to clear herself. Speak up, prisoner, ef you've got anything ter say."

"I've got nothing to say," said Lowrey, "except that the woman is innocent. I think you're makin' a mistake, an' that you'll be sorry fer what you're going to do. A man is sometimes justified in killing another."

"A nigger is never justified in killin' a white man," said Peebles. "That's the onwritten law of the Southe'n States."

"Durn the law," said Skinner, impatiently, pulling the rope uncomfortably tight. "Shall we swing him up now, boys?"

"*Hol'* on a minute," interposed Peebles. "Don't be in sech a' all-fired hurry. This here ain't no corn-shuckin' match. There' lots o' time; it's early in the evenin' yet. Mebbe the nigger would like to pray. I sorter think we ought to ask the divine blessin' on the whole thing anyhow. It's a little onreg'lar, but the end jestifies the means. Who'll offer pra'r?"

No one volunteered. Skinner ripped out an impatient oath.

"Shet up that cussin', Jeff," continued Peebles. "It's onseemly. There's several pillars o' the chu'ch here. Who'll lead in pra'r?"

"Never you min' who's here," growled one of the mob, with an eye to possible consequences. "I don't know a soul in this party. My eyesight's po' and my memory's failin', so I can't recollect one day whar I wuz the night befo'."

"I saw a preacher a few minutes ago," said another. "Wait till I see if I can find him."

He darted off and in a minute or two returned, dragging Elder Gadson by the arm, more dead than alive.

"Come along, elder," he cried. "We're holdin' a little necktie party, an' we need yo'r services. We want you to lead in prayer for the soul of the murderer of Bob Utley."

Chapter 22

*W*hen Lowrey had left the school-house at three o'clock on Friday, Rose Amelia had followed him until he reached the edge of the town, and there she had stopped, intending to wait until nightfall for his return, as she could not very well follow him unperceived through the town. When it became dark she ran back home for her supper, and then went out and waited in vain for Lowrey to pass along the road, until sleepiness overpowered her, and she nodded. She woke up a few minutes later, and, not knowing how long she had slept, thought perhaps he had gone by; so she went home disconsolately to bed.

She slept a little late the next morning, and as she opened her eyes on waking she heard, through the chinks between the logs of the house, her mother and a neighbor talking in animated tones.

"Fer Gawd's sake, chile, yo' doan mean ter tell me."

"Yas, I does. It's de truf sho's yer bawn. Give hisse'f up, and was put right in jail."

"Well, nobody knows w'at gwine ter happen! Wouldn' be'n mo' 'stonish' ef de moon had fell down."

"Well, good-bye, honey. I's got ter run along an' tell some mo' folks." And the gossiping neighbor rushed away.

Rose Amelia had pricked up her ears as she caught the last few words of the conversation, and a terrible fear assailed her—so terrible indeed that for a little while she seemed turned to stone. Her mother came running in.

"Shug, O Shug, wake up dar an' listen ter de noos. W'at yer reckon?"

"W'at is it, mammy? Tell me quick," she stammered, with ashen cheeks and starting eyes.

"Yo' teacher, Mr. Lowrey, has done b'en an' gone an' give hisse'f up fer murd'rin' Marse Bob Utley. 'Fo' de Lawd, chile, I can't 'splain ter myse'f w'at fer he do dat. But w'at de matter wid yer, chile?"

Rose Amelia had fallen into a fit. She had always been "fittified," as her mother would have expressed it, so her mother was not seriously alarmed. She laid her back on the bed, applied a few simple remedies, and then went about her household duties.

The paroxysm was soon over, and in about an hour Rose Amelia recovered consciousness. She managed to dress herself—the operation was simple—and her mother gave her a cup of coffee, after drinking which she went out, and proceeded straight through the town to the jail where her dear teacher was confined. She stood off at a distance and looked at its stern, forbidding brick walls and barred windows. She was familiar with the place. Her father had often been in jail, and she had not thought of it as being a great hardship in his case. But it was different with her teacher; she had put him on a pedestal, had worshipped him as a god, and now her idol had fallen by her own hand. For she divined that he had given himself up for love of the hated white woman. She threw herself on the ground and wept bitterly, and, when the paroxysm of her grief was over, relapsed into the apathy of despair. With these alternations of mood the long day wore slowly away.

Towards evening hunger drove her homeward. But in going through the town she heard Lowrey's name mentioned. She forgot her hunger, and hung around the town to hear what might be said of him. She saw the crowd collected on the sidewalk, and slipping along the walls of the houses, behind boxes and barrels, with all her faculties on the alert, she came near enough to learn the fearful truth.

They were going to kill her teacher—her teacher whom she loved so dearly! His kind eyes would look no more upon Rose Amelia, his dear voice no longer guide her poor mind in its gropings after knowledge! In the dark night he would die, by the hands of cruel strangers, with no friend to comfort, no hand to clasp, as he felt his way across the dark river of death! And he could not think one kind thought of poor Rose

Amelia in his last hour, for it was she to whom he owed his fate! Rather would he curse her with his dying breath and blast her with his look, for she, she only was to blame for his fate!

With this turmoil in her heart Rose Amelia, drawn by a resistless impulse, had followed the lynching party when they started on their murderous mission, keeping out of sight, but near enough to see and hear much of what was going on.

She saw them enter the jail-yard, and a little later come out; and by the light of the moon she saw, as they passed through the open, the figure of her teacher, manacled, surrounded by armed men with bearded faces. To her wild imagination they seemed like devils, and Lowrey like a lost soul in their clutches. Fascinated she watched them, and unconsciously drew nearer, until she stood just within the shadow of the trees encircling the space where the mob had gathered for the culmination of their crime. When she saw the rope placed around his neck, she could endure no more, but with a wild and inarticulate cry turned and fled into the night. On and on she ran; she could not go far enough to shut out that dreadful sight. It seemed to follow her. Now it must be all over, and in the shadow of the oak his lifeless form must be hanging, and his fixed eyes staring, staring, staring at Rose Amelia, with a reproachfulness which would not cease even in death.

A day or two later some negroes hunting in the swamp found the body of a little black girl lying face downward, in a pool of stagnant ooze in which it was partially embedded. Whether Rose had fallen in a fit, and in the helplessness of unconsciousness had perished; or whether she had run until exhausted, and falling, had not had strength enough left to extricate herself; or whether in her remorse and despair she had taken her own life, no one of course could know. Her narrow brain, with the great passion it had yet been large enough to foster, and with all the lesser feelings which had grown around and fed upon the master passion, had found rest from its throbbing; the woman's heart in the child's stunted frame was stilled forever, and Rose Amelia had expiated her sin.

Chapter 23

When Elder Gadson was drawn into the circle of lynchers, he saw vaguely outlined in the shadow of the old oak, what he supposed to be the figure of Mandy Oxendine. It was too dark under the tree for the eye to distinguish clearly the outlines of the silent figure standing there. But the line of new Manila rope running up into the tree above, and the face at the lower end of it were dimly visible by the contrast of their whiteness with the surrounding gloom. There was no opportunity for closer observation to reveal his mistake, and indeed so vividly had the elder's imagination pictured the scene that it is doubtful that anything but broad daylight would have dispelled his illusion. But to still further lessen his chances of being undeceived, after the first look a sudden wave of feeling swept up from his heart, suffused his cheek and dimmed his eye, and for the next few moments the struggle in his own bosom shut out the world so that he seemed to see it as through a veil of mist.

"Parson," said Peebles, "we 'uns is vistin' the extreme penalty o' the law, a leetle in advance p'raps, and p'raps a leetle onreglar, on the murderer o' Bob Utley, an' we wants you to lead us in pra'r befo' we finish the job."

"But there has been no trial," stammered the elder, "the murderer has never been convicted."

"The prisoner has confessed, an' will be hung anyhow, so we're only savin' the country onnecessary expense. Come, Elder, invoke the divine blessin'. We'll dispense with the sermon."

"Yas, hurry up, Elder, we're gittin' tired. It's our bedtime, and every las' one of us wants to git ter bed at the reg'lar hour to-night. We're all spendin' the evenin' peaceably at home."

Elder Gadson, thus apostrophized, knelt down upon the ground. He did not notice that he had knelt upon a rough spot; and he did not feel the sharp projections that pressed upon his knees and at another time would have given him exquisite pain.

"Oh, God," he cried, "the Father of us all, Thou who didst make us, and didst ordain our course here below, Thou who knowest our weaknesses, Thou who knowest how hard we strive and how far we fall short of what Thou wouldst have us to be, pardon this poor sinner who has strayed so far from the path of duty, who has suffered a worldly love to draw his heart from thy high service of saving souls."

The profound emotion revealed by the preacher's accents, and the unaccustomed eloquence of his words had fixed the attention of the mob, so much so that even Skinner for a moment forgot his hurry, and relaxed somewhat his hold upon the rope, so that Lowrey was able to breathe freely. And even the prisoner, struck by the passionate utterance of the preacher, forgot for a moment his own impending doom and listened. The preacher's last words had aroused something more than attention; they had awakened in the minds of the crowd a wondering curiosity, so that as the preacher went on, all heads were bent forward to catch his words.

"Thou who knowest the secrets of all hearts, knowest how and why thy servant, thine unworthy servant hath sinned, and shed the blood of his fellow-man. Thou knowest, that though the deed may not have been an unjust one, the underlyin' motive was not one which would find favor in thy sight."

Perfect silence in the circle, and the sounds of the night—the shrill chirp of the cicada, and the distant croaking of frogs—seemed but to make the silence more intense, and to form a fitting accompaniment to the tragedy that was being enacted under the autumn sky. The preacher went on, and his voice was a wail of agony.

"And, now, O God, give thine unworthy servant strength to confess the truth, to save the innocent, and to put himself in the place of the one who has been unjustly accused. And while his life shall go out at the hand of these self-constituted ministers of vengeance, have mercy on the poor sin-tortured soul which shall come before thee, red with a brother's blood."

As the preacher said this he rose; and the listening mob, who were awaiting something, they knew not what, pressed closer, so as to lose no word and no inflection of his voice.

"Yes, gentlemen," he cried, throwing aloft his hands with a familiar pulpit gesture, "the prisoner whom you are about to hurry into the presence of God is innocent. I and I alone committed this crime; my hand, and mine alone, struck the blow that slew Robert Utley. I loved this woman. I saw him with her. I followed them. He assaulted her; I killed him. Most men in my place would have done the same. But I do not seek to justify myself. Take my worthless life, for it will be of no more use to me or any one else. Take it now I beg of you, for if you spare it for but one hour I shall want to cling to it."

For a moment the mob was confounded. Then the reaction came.

"Gentlemen," said Peebles, "you see the advantage o' not bein' in a hurry. It 'pears to me we come mighty nigh hangin' a' innocent man."

"I don't know about that," said McAllister. "The other one has confessed too."

"The gal has confessed," said the jailer, who came forward from the place where he had been a concealed though interested witness of the whole proceeding.

This staggered them. They moved closer to Lowrey.

"Did you kill him?" they asked.

"I did not," he said. "I thought she did, and I was willing to take her place."

They stood around irresolutely. The preacher meantime had fallen into a sort of stupor, and had not yet realized that it was not Mandy whom he had seen standing under the tree. He came to himself with a start and rushing forward asked—

"Is she free?"

"Is who free?" said McAllister. "The nigger? No, we ain't got our bearin's yet."

"The girl—is she free?"

"No," said several voices, "she's in jail all right enough."

The preacher was speechless with amazement.

"Well," said Skinner in tones of impatience mingled with disgust, "what are we goin' to do? I come out her to do somethin'. Shall we hang the nigger?"

"Not if he didn't kill Utley," answered Peebles.

"I dunno," said Skinner stubbornly. "Pears like a pity ter buy this rope an' break our night's res' fer nuthin'. It's true the nigger didn' kill Utley, but he said he did, an' it kind er goes ag'in the grain fer me ter hear a nigger even *say* he killed a white man."

"*Don't* be so onpatient, Jeff," said Peebles. "We ain't goin' ter hang the wrong man just to please you, even if he is a nigger. After all, he's a pretty white nigger. You kin save that rope; you may have a use fer it some other time."

"What's the matter," said a gruff voice from the outskirts of the crowd, "with hangin' the preacher?"

"No, gentlemen," said Peebles with emphasis, "I purtest ag'in the si'gestion. Every man should have a fair trial and have his guilt passed on by a jury before he is convicted of a crime. The right to trial by jury is one o' the bull-works of our libbutty. Mebbe the preacher wuz jestified in killin' him. We'll pos'pone the hangin' fer ternight, and lock 'em both up, an' let the officers o' the law 'rastle with the problem, fer there's evidently some myst'ry somewhar."

The mob then dispersed, a sufficient number returning to the jail to escort Lowrey and the preacher, who were both locked up by the jailer.

Chapter 24

The next day the three prisoners were brought before a magistrate and a preliminary examination was held to ascertain the facts of Utley's murder. The whole story came out, and in order to explain the connection of Lowrey with the affair, his hitherto secret relations with Mandy became a matter of public knowledge, as did also the fact of her origin and her connection with the colored race. This cleared up many difficulties. The fact that Mandy was colored justified Lowrey's attentions; that she was supposed to be white explained the preacher's interest; and her youth, her sex and her beauty excused in Mandy what would ordinarily have been regarded as an almost unpardonable social crime—the breaking of caste and the intrusion of one tainted by base blood into the ranks of the white people.

Mandy and Lowrey were discharged from custody. Elder Gadson was committed to prison, to await the action of the grand jury. In due time he was indicted, and tried. During his confinement his love of life had regained the ascendancy, and having found some friends who were willing to help him, he secured the services of a good lawyer. When the case came on he entered the plea of not guilty; and having succeeded in convincing the jury that he had slain Robert Utley in self-defense, he was acquitted on the first ballot. He went to South Carolina, and after a short interval, resumed his evangelistic labors, which he prosecuted with much of his old zeal and success. He married a mature woman of settled habits, and no longer takes other than a pastoral interest in the ewe lambs of his various flocks.

After their terrible experience Mandy and Tom were drawn even more closely to each other; and since Mandy's secret had become known, there was no longer any reason for concealment, and Lowrey could go to see her and enjoy openly the lover's privileges he had hitherto only snatched by stealth.

He finished out his school, which lasted but two weeks longer. He adjourned school one afternoon for poor Rose Amelia's funeral. And as he stood by the rude pine coffin and looked down upon the wizened features, still more contracted in death, he dropped a tear at the thought that here lay one who had been fond of him. And while he never knew how much she had loved him, he always kept in his memory a little corner for poor Rose Amelia.

After the trial and acquittal of Elder Gadson, at which Mandy and Tom appeared as witnesses and attracted much notice, they went away to their former home, where they were married among the friends of their youth. With their after life this record of their period of storm and stress has nothing to do. They were young enough to have much hope for the future, and much faith in themselves; and in the glow of youth and satisfied love the gloom of their recent tragic experiences soon wore away. Whether they went to the North, where there was larger opportunity and a more liberal environment, and remaining true to their own people, in spite of some scorn and some isolation, found a measurable degree of contentment and happiness; or whether they chose to sink their past in the gulf of oblivion, and sought in the great white world such a place as their talents and their virtues merited, it is not for this chronicle to relate. They deserved to be happy; but we do not all get our deserts, as many a lucky rogue may congratulate himself, and as many an ill-used honest man can testify.

The End

Charles Hackenberry is an associate professor of English at Pennsylvania State University, Altoona Campus, where he teaches literature and writing. His 1984 essay "Meaning and Models" in *American Literary Realism* marked the beginning of his work on Charles Chesnutt's unpublished manuscripts. In addition to scholarly articles, Hackenberry has published two novels.

William L. Andrews is E. Maynard Adams Professor of English at the University of North Carolina at Chapel Hill. He is the author of *The Literary Career of Charles W. Chesnutt* (1980) and *To Tell a Free Story: The First Century of Afro-American Autobiography, 1760–1865* (1986) and the editor of the *Norton Anthology of African American Literature* (1997) and *The Oxford Companion to African American Literature* (1997), among other works.